For — J.

All my best!

The Pet Washer

By

JENNIFER LYNN ALVAREZ

Jnfr L. Ay

www.thepetwasher.com

Dream Big

Cover Design by Zeolight

Library of Congress Control Number: 2012944593
ISBN 978-0-9848484-5-4

~For Nick, Crystal, David, and the Pets

Table of Contents

~Prologue~

A DOOR OPENED, releasing a sliver of light and a small girl onto a darkened street. The girl, bundled in a thick jacket, stepped onto the sidewalk. She shut the door behind her, blackening the street once more. Cianna shivered. Spring mornings were cold in the port town of Flores, and she was up and out before the sun today. The salty breeze off the Borgan Sea ruffled her long red hair.

Cianna extended her cane and headed north toward Port Street. The dark morning didn't bother her; she'd been born blind. Cianna was already ticking off the things she needed to do at work. It was spring, the busiest time of year for the pet washers in Flores. Cianna was low on pet shampoo and ear cleaner. Since she didn't use store-bought products, she'd have to mix up two batches before the Pet Palace opened at eight.

Cianna knew the way to work by heart. She'd memorized every uneven step on the sidewalk, every protruding porch, every signpost. She mindlessly swept her cane ahead of her, a long-standing habit ingrained by her father, even though he wasn't watching her now.

Cianna reached Port Street and turned left. She heard a pair of carriage horses trot past her. It was the morning newspaper delivery. Cianna sniffed the air. Flowers were in full bloom, coffee was brewing somewhere, rough smoke filtered out of the chimneys, and the smell of hay and horses lingered heavily near the town stable.

When Cianna arrived at work, the owner, Mr. Talley, was already there and the front door was unlocked. She slipped upstairs to her washing room, hung up her coat, and tied on her apron. She opened her jars of ingredients, and dove into the long workday ahead of her. Cianna had no idea that, within a few hours, a chance meeting and the color of her hair would change her life forever.

One

~The Princess~

THIS IS BAD NEWS," Polly said to her little dog, Leroy. He was asleep next to her on the window seat. Leroy was black and tan, and spoiled rotten. Polly kept his long silky bangs clipped in a pink bow. He was her favorite pet and he knew it. The rest of her dogs lived in a large kennel behind the stable. Leroy lived with Polly in the castle.

"I know you're awake," Polly accused him. Leroy yawned and peeked at her. She pulled him onto her lap.

"Look at this letter." Polly unfolded a note written on glitter paper. She held it in front of his eyes as though he could read it himself. Leroy sniffed the paper and sneezed. "Gross!" Polly cried. She snatched it away from him and wiped the note dry with a lace handkerchief. "I'll read it to you."

Dearest Polly,
Princess Mirabel has come down
with the pox. She is not permitted
to leave our castle for two weeks.
We regret to inform you that
she will not be able to perform
at the Spring Festival this year.
Regards, Queen Bridgette

Polly's mother, Adeline, had tucked the note on her breakfast tray. "What am I going to do, Leroy?" Polly groaned. "Who will dance Mirabel's part in my performance?"

Polly and her family were vacationing with all the other royal families on the island of Windym. It was spring break! For six long weeks, the kings and queens would relax from the hard work of ruling their separate kingdoms while their children enjoyed a break from school.

The seven royal families looked forward to visiting their second castles all winter, and Polly's family lived in the largest one. The year-round castle workers had made sure the royal pantries were stocked with food and the second homes were clean and ready for their owners.

As soon as their ships anchored, Polly and her royal friends flocked to their second bedrooms to see what toys or clothes they might have left behind the year before. Dusting off their swords and slippers, they readied themselves for endless parties, sleepovers, trips to town, and the highlight of the season—the Spring Festival.

Non-royal families from Windym and nearby kingdoms could purchase tickets to view the different tournaments or to attend the dance, but the tickets were expensive.

Right now, sitting with Leroy, Polly could only think of one thing—her dance performance. The dance, called *The Seven Sisters*, had been advertised in the town newspaper, and the princesses had been practicing for many weeks. Mirabel's illness left Polly with only six dancers. If she didn't find another girl soon, she would have to cancel the performance. Polly shuddered.

There were other princesses to choose from, but Polly was picky. Her entire dance was color-coded, from the hair to the dresses to the shoes. The idea of two girls performing with the same hair color made her skin crawl.

Mirabel had dark red hair, so Polly would have to find a girl with that color to replace her. The only other redheaded princess in Windym was six months old. Polly sighed. She had two weeks to find a red-haired girl, make friends with her, and teach her the dance.

"I might have to use Princess Katie," she told Leroy. Katie had light yellow hair, but Polly would dye it red if she had to. Katie was a year younger than Polly, but she wasn't pretty.

While it was false that *all* princesses were beautiful, some truly were, and Polly only befriended them. It wasn't something she thought about; she simply enjoyed beautiful things and surrounded herself with them— from her dogs to her shoes to her hair clips. Polly also happened to be beautiful herself, and she lured many princesses (and princes) into following her every command.

"I will have to figure this out this later," Polly decided, still talking to Leroy, who was snoring now. "But first, I have another problem." Polly hadn't yet picked out her Spring Festival gown. Every year she wore the best dress to the dance, and every year she was featured on the cover of *Princess Style* magazine.

Dress rumors were galloping across the island faster than the princes raced their ponies, and it was said Princess Lexi had a fantastic dress from her homeland of Manlaya. Everyone knew the finest fabrics in all of the seven kingdoms were woven there.

Lexi was Polly's best friend, sort of. She was in the dance and she was pretty, but she was always trying to outdo her. Polly frowned. She needed to find a truly special dress or Lexi would end up on the cover of *Princess Style* magazine instead of her.

"Leroy, I have to go shopping today!" Polly shoved her dog off her lap and he landed on the floor with a sharp yelp. "Sorry," she said with a quick pat on his head. She would ride to the dressmaking shops in Flores and keep her eye out for a red-haired girl. The girl didn't have to be a princess, she just had to be perfect!

Polly walked into her clothes closet and chose the new riding outfit she'd received for her twelfth birthday. The breeches were white with violet stripes down the sides, and the shirt was made of white lace and decorated with violet ribbons. Polly pulled on her black riding boots, her black gloves, and tied her curls back with a violet ribbon. All ready now, she skipped out the door. Leroy crawled into a miniature canopy bed, the exact replica of Polly's, and went back to sleep.

"Mother!" shouted Princess Polly from the top of the stairs.

"Please don't yell in the castle," answered Queen Adeline from the first floor.

"Okay!" said the princess, still shouting. "Let's ride into town. I want to go dress shopping!" Polly slid down the rail and landed neatly on her feet at the bottom of the marble staircase.

"Goodness, Polly," her mother scolded. "You must calm down." The regal queen was also dressed for riding. She was tall and her hair was black, but cut short. And unlike Polly, who had light blue eyes, Adeline's were brown. "I already ordered the horses," she said. "Did you forget that I'm taking you to the Seaside for lunch today?"

The blasted note from Queen Bridgette had ruined her morning and Polly had forgotten. She flashed her mother a charming smile. "Let's shop *and* get lunch!"

"Deal!" agreed the queen. Polly was strong willed, stubborn, and she drove Adeline crazy, but she adored her only child all the same. They held gloved hands and walked outside together.

The gentle heat of the spring sun greeted them. Polly took a deep, long breath, her troubles forgotten for the moment. The meadow surrounding her castle was full of flowers, colorful songbirds decorated the trees, and the last of the snow had melted into the bubbling creek that fed their pond. Frogs croaked loudly on the large, flat lily pads. At the forest edge, she spotted a red fox and her kits chasing bugs. The entire island of Windym was blazing with new life. Polly's homeland, Amerok, was still covered in snow.

Caden, the stable boy, waited with their horses at the front door. Polly almost didn't recognize him. He'd grown a lot in a year. His hair was longer, bleached by the sun, and his face had lost its roundness. His shoulders were broad from stacking hay and his strong jaw was covered in blond stubble. He no longer resembled the boy she liked to boss around.

Queen Adeline mounted her gray mare, Mina. Polly turned from Caden and gaped at the horse saddled for her. It was Gildon. The brown gelding—the *plain* brown gelding! She scowled at Caden, and he looked at her with the same green eyes he'd had since boyhood. She would not take this treatment from him or anyone! Polly stood as tall as she could and pointed hard at Gildon. "I am *not* riding that horse. Bring me Tiara."

Adeline wiped her brow. She wished her daughter were not so picky and rude. Caden hesitated.

"Bring me Tiara," Polly repeated.

Caden tried to change her mind. "Polly, Tiara needs a lot more training before she'll be a safe riding horse. Take Gildon, he's trustworthy."

Polly fumed. She was a good rider, and she could handle Tiara. She would not change her mind. "Everyone in Windym is shopping today. I can't be seen on a boring brown horse. Bring me Tiara." Her blue eyes flashed.

Caden gave up. He led Gildon back to the stable, and fifteen minutes later he returned with Tiara.

Princess Polly's eyes lit up at the sight of her pretty mare. Tiara was as white as snow. Her long mane and tail curled in loose ringlets and were highlighted with streaks of silver hair. Her eyes were large and black. Even as a foal, royals had traveled to the pink castle to watch Tiara play in the fields. She was, hands down, the best-looking horse on the island, and perhaps in the seven kingdoms.

Tiara pranced in place, her head high, her neck arched. Polly noticed Caden had taken the time to paint Tiara's hooves violet to match her new riding outfit. *That's more like it*, she thought. She decided to forgive him for saddling Gildon first.

Caden helped Polly mount her horse. "Go slow, Princess," Caden warned her. "She's fresh from eating the spring grass." Spring grass was full of sugar. It could make even a calm horse hyper, and Tiara was already not a calm horse. Caden wished Polly would ride

Gildon. Tiara had more ene
mistress needed.

Polly grinned. "No worries, Cau
handle her. Are you ready, Mama?"
didn't wait for an answer. She pointed Tiai.
toward Flores and smacked her with the riding
whip. Tiara reared back on her hind legs and
bolted across the meadow. Polly's scream
ricocheted through the valley. She let go of the
whip and wrapped her fists in Tiara's mane,
hanging on for dear life as the mare thundered
toward Flores.

"That girl!" moaned the queen. Adeline
kicked her mare and chased after Polly. Caden
shook his head. Tiara was also the fastest
horse in Windym, Adeline wouldn't catch her.
Still shaking his head, Caden walked back to
the stable.

Tiara galloped across the meadow, into the
woods, over a stream, and then down the
country road all the way to Flores. Adeline
followed at a canter, unable and unwilling to
ride at the same breakneck pace. All the way
she feared she would come across her
daughter fallen on the ground, injured or
worse. Finally, the two mares came to a sliding
stop at the town gates.

"Are you all right, Polly?" the queen asked.
Adeline's horse, Mina, was out of breath and

steaming sweat. Tiara was still dry. Her large eyes glittered with pleasure.

Polly gasped for air. "I'm fine, Mother," she choked. She patted her horse. "I wanted to run, didn't I, Tiara?"

Adeline only cared that Polly was okay. She didn't expect her stubborn daughter to admit she was scared. "Then let's go shopping," said the queen. They trotted through the gates of Flores side by side.

Still fiery, Tiara pranced down the cobblestone streets, flicking her sassy tail. Polly relaxed. The townsfolk paused to watch them pass. *Everyone wishes they were me*, she thought.

Two
~The Pet Washer~

AS POLLY AND ADELINE rode down Port Street in Flores, Cianna was working hard at the Royal Pet Palace and Day Spa. She was one of three pet washers who worked there. The Pampered Pet, on Beach Street, employed two pet washers, but Cianna was the best of them all. The royals often asked for her by name.

Right now she was scrubbing a large pooch that had been sprayed by a skunk. Cianna had a perfect nose for all odors, both fine and foul. She could identify ten different types of dirt and mud, thirty types of plants, sixteen types of poisons, countless household odors, and six conditions of bad breath. She could also detect skin allergies and sicknesses in pets.

Cianna was popular because she didn't just wash the pets; she treated the conditions that made them smell bad in the first place. She brushed teeth, changed diets, and treated skin diseases—all with her own homemade soaps, lotions, toothpastes, and medicines. The royals in Windym loved their pets very much. Cianna's work pleased them and this pleased Cianna's boss, Mr. Talley.

Cianna scrubbed the skunk smell out of the big dog named Hank. His hair felt rough to her fingers. She frowned, Hank usually had soft hair. She opened his mouth and smelled his breath. "Aha!" Cianna said. "You've been eating sweets again, Hank." She smelled cinnamon icing and vanilla. His owner, Princess Laci, liked to feed him sweets from her table, and sweets were not good for Hank. The sugars caused his teeth and hair to become dry and brittle.

Cianna went to her little kitchen and lifted a twenty-pound bag of her homemade dog food. She added the nutrients that would restore Hank's hair and strengthen his teeth. She mixed them all together and sealed the bag. She went downstairs and asked Mia, her friend and ex-babysitter, to write a note to attach to the bag. The note read:

Dearest Princess Laci,
Hank's hair is breaking again.
I made a special dog food for him.

*Please feed him ½ cup of food
twice a day for four weeks.
Please limit dessert to
only once per week.
Yours, Cianna*

Cianna went back to the large tub where Hank was leashed. Worried about cavities from all the sugar, she brushed his teeth. Afterward, she sprayed Hank with a leave-in conditioner then massaged it deep into his fur. She sniffed the air and smiled, now Hank smelled like strawberries and melons.

Cianna finger-curled his long fur and set it with pins. She led him to a mat to lie down and she tossed him a mint-flavored bone to chew while his hair dried. Jolee would arrive soon to pick him up. Jolee was even more popular with the royal families than Cianna. She colored, dyed, and painted the pets' furs. She was famous in Windym and in the seven kingdoms for her animal artwork.

Jolee painted patterns, prints, 3-D pictures, masks, written messages, camouflage, landscapes … really she could paint anything on a pet. Today she was going to color Hank's long hair bright yellow. Hank was attending a lemonade party with Princess Laci, and since everyone wears yellow to a lemonade party, so would Hank.

Cianna patted the dog and sighed. "You smell good and you feel good, Hank. I just wish I could see you." Hank whimpered, and Cianna scratched his ears. "Don't cry." She walked away to clean her tub. Cianna had decided a long time ago not to feel sorry for herself.

She heard a bell ring. It was Mr. Talley, the owner of the Royal Pet Palace and Day Spa. His office was near the front desk, and he used the bell to call meetings. All the workers in the Pet Palace scurried to his office. Cianna felt her way down the stairs, taking two at a time. Of the forty men, women, girls, and boys who worked at the Pet Palace, Cianna was the first to arrive. Her blindness had never been an excuse for tardiness!

Mr. Talley waited for everyone to quiet down. "As you know, this is the busiest time of the year," he announced. "The Spring Dance is two weeks away. We are going to be flooded with appointments from now until then."

The workers nodded to one another. It was well-known that the royals brought their pets to the dances. None of the workers had ever been to the Spring Dance because the tickets were too expensive. Only the royals and the wealthy shop owners could afford to attend. Mr. Talley and his wife had already purchased their tickets.

Mr. Talley continued. "As usual, we will work seven days a week until the day of the festival. Pay attention to what you're doing. We cannot have any mistakes like we had last week."

Cianna heard feet shuffling, and someone coughed. Last week one of the colorists had mixed her colors without paying attention. Her name was Lizzy. She'd meant to dye a horse's mane and tail blue, but she added too much bitterroot. She applied the dye to the horse's hair and waited twenty minutes. When she rinsed it out, the long tail hair broke in half.

The owner of the horse, Prince Jayson, wanted Mr. Talley to fire Lizzy. The palomino was his jousting horse for the spring games, and Prince Jayson would look silly riding a horse with only half a tail! Mr. Talley appeased Jayson by giving the horse free spidersilk hair extensions. Jolee dyed the tail royal blue to match the prince's jousting jacket. Of course, Mr. Talley did not ask the prince to pay for any of this. The prince was happy, but Mr. Talley was not pleased. Spidersilk hair extensions were expensive.

Mr. Talley didn't fire Lizzy, but he suspended her and sent her to night classes to re-learn how to mix her dyes. Everyone at the Pet Palace felt sorry for her. She was missing out on all the extra money they earned during the spring season. The work was hard and the days were long, but the royals tipped well. During the six weeks of spring break, the workers made four times their normal pay!

Mr. Talley flipped through his notes. "The Pampered Pet is offering coupons and lower prices this year," he warned. The Pampered Pet was located by the Seaside restaurant on Beach Street, and they were Mr. Talley's fiercest competition. "I won't lower my prices, but we will be offering extra services for free for the next two weeks."

Mr. Talley rustled through his papers. "Here they are: All massages will last an extra fifteen minutes. All hoof and claw painters will use scented polish at no extra charge. All pet washings will include a deep conditioning treatment. All hair and fur styles will include super-shine spray. All colorists will include scent and glitter in their dyes at no extra charge. All beauty treatments will include a free paw, leg, or wing massage."

Someone groaned.

"Understood?" Mr. Talley asked.

"Yes, sir," they all agreed.

"Great, let's get back to work!"

The workers headed back to their jobs. Cianna was curious. All her life she'd heard about the Spring Dance, and she dreamed of twirling to the music in a soft, full dress. Cianna loved her job, but it was hard for her to hear about all the fun knowing she wouldn't attend.

"What are you thinking about, Cianna?" Mia asked. Mia was the receptionist at the Royal Pet Palace and Day Spa. The two had known each other since Cianna was a little girl.

"Nothing," she answered. Cianna had a short break in her schedule, so she decided to eat lunch early. "Mia, I'm going to run home. I'll be back soon."

"Okay, your next appointment is in half an hour."

Cianna left the Pet Palace and walked home. She held her walking cane in her hand, but she didn't use it. She lived two blocks away on Laurel Lane. Cianna rented a tiny apartment above the perfume shop, and she loved her home because it always smelled good. Her building was one of the tallest in Flores, it had five stories, and Cianna's apartment was on the top floor.

Cianna lived there by herself. After her father's ship disappeared when she was eight, she'd lived with Mia for a few years. Later, she discovered the apartment. Cianna had also attended the Country Day School for a while, but the teachers didn't know what to do with a blind student. Cianna couldn't see the chalkboard and she couldn't read or write.

Cianna began skipping school to go to work with Mia at the Pet Palace. After a few months of begging, Mr. Talley agreed to let her wash some of the pets. The rest was history. Cianna formulated her own shampoos, treated for fleas, and brushed teeth. She became so popular with the customers that Mr. Talley hired her, and she never went back to the Country Day School after that. While she longed to read and write, she knew it was impossible. Instead, she became the best pet washer on the island.

Cianna, now fourteen, was done being a burden to Mia—even though Mia insisted she wasn't. When she heard about the tiny apartment for rent above the perfume shop, Cianna took it and moved in the same day. That was a year ago.

The best thing about her new home was the large window. It overlooked the sea and the coast of Windym. Of course, Cianna couldn't see out of it, but she loved to open the window and take in all the scents of the land. The smell of the Borgan Sea was always there. The other smells changed depending on the time of year.

Cianna counted the seasons by the scents in the air. She could smell the dryness of the leaves in fall, feel the rain before it fell, detect the first blooms of spring before they opened, and sense the withering death of the grass in summer.

She could track the local wildlife in the nearby forest too. The pungent odor of the skunks and the urine from cougar spray were easy to identify. She heard the piercing whistle of hawks, the scurrying of field mice, and the chattering of coyotes. Quite often the scents of recently washed pets drifted to her from the sidewalks.

She could distinguish her own clients from the animals washed at the Pampered Pet because she didn't mask bad odors with perfume like they did. She treated her clients from the inside out. Cianna also enjoyed the sweet smells from the bakeries, the salty tang from the piers, and the smoky flavors wafting from the restaurants.

Cianna didn't have much time to eat and get back to work. She climbed the last of the steps, unlocked her apartment, and walked inside her tiny home. She pulled some cheese out of her cooler, cut a piece of bread, and poured a glass of milk, carrying everything on a tray to her favorite seat by the big window. It was open, and she enjoyed the soft breeze on her face.

Cianna couldn't wait for the evening of the Spring Dance. It was held every year at Sweet Hall outside of Flores. Because she was in the tallest building and Sweet Hall was on the tallest hill, Cianna was in the perfect position to hear every sound that echoed across the little valley.

The best musicians and singers in the seven kingdoms performed at the dance. She was downwind of the hill, and her tongue could almost taste the delicious-smelling food.

Cianna knew she would never attend this wonderful festival, but she dreamed about touching the lovely dresses, munching on the sweet pastries, and feeling the coldness of the ice sculptures. She wanted to pet all the royal animals that she worked so hard to clean, but most of all, Cianna wanted to laugh with friends and maybe dance with a boy.

Cianna finished her daydream and her lunch and headed back to work. Once there, she climbed the stairs to her grooming room. She could smell an animal in the waiting area. It was her next appointment.

"Hi, Trixi," she said. Trixi was a nervous little cheetah. She belonged to Princess Mirabel, but Mirabel's brother, Prince Luke, used her for hunting. Trixi chased deer for him while he tried to shoot them with his bow. Luckily, he was a terrible shot.

First, Cianna examined Trixi. She was filthy with thick mud caked inside her paws. This appointment was going to take a while. Trixi, like most cheetahs, hated water. Cianna had invented a special shampoo that could be applied dry, and her dry baths were one of the reasons why she was just as popular with the pets as she was with their owners.

Cianna got to work washing Trixi. The cheetah also needed a leave-in conditioning treatment, two bottles of Cianna's Stomach Tonic, and Minty Treats. The cheetah purred, pleased to have the mud out of her toes. Cianna applied the leave-in conditioner to Trixi's coat and led her to the drying area. Hank had already been taken by Jolee. Trixi leaned into Cianna, tickling her face with her whiskers. Cianna kissed the cheetah's nose and told her to be good.

Mr. Talley popped into her room. "You have six clients waiting downstairs, Cianna."

Cianna sighed. "I'm ready." She loved her job, but she wished she didn't have to rush. If she could, she would spend hours with each animal, but this time of year that was impossible. Cianna rubbed lotion into her red, cracked hands and braced herself for the rest of the day.

Three

~*Mystery Cloth*~

PRINCESS POLLY and her mother rode to the finest dress shop in Flores, called the Satin Ribbon. "Good day, Queen Adeline. Good day, Princess Polly," greeted Mrs. Dunkins, the owner of the Satin Ribbon. She curtsied to Polly and her mother. They were her best customers, but they were also the hardest for her to please.

Mrs. Dunkins snapped her fingers at her assistant, Sasha, and pointed to the royal horses. Sasha rushed outside and led the horses to the town stable. There they would be unsaddled, rinsed, and fed a hot bran mash while the ladies shopped. Since they were royal horses, they would also be rubbed down and allowed to relax in large, clean box stalls.

Polly watched the mares leave with Sasha. She was proud of her family's horses, except for Gildon. She'd forgotten all about the crazy ride into town, and at least no one had seen her mare's bad behavior. Next time she would not ride Tiara with a whip.

"How may I help Your Highnesses today?" asked Mrs. Dunkins.

Polly answered, "I want to see your fabrics, Mrs. Dunkins. My dress this year has to be the best ever if I'm going to make the cover of *Princess Style* again. I hear that Princess Lexi will be wearing something just invented."

"I have some lovely new fabrics for you, Your Highness," said Mrs. Dunkins. She went into her storeroom to hide her distress from the royal ladies. She did not have a fabulous new fabric for Polly. She was expecting a shipment from Manlaya, but it was late. Sasha returned from taking the horses to the stable, and she helped Mrs. Dunkins look through the bolts of cloth in the storeroom.

Polly and Adeline browsed through the dresses on the racks. Adeline held up a turquoise gown. It was slim-fitting and trimmed with green lace. "This one's pretty," she said.

"Gross, Mom!" Polly gagged.

"I think it's nice." The queen continued to flip through dresses. Adeline held up another one. It was red with a full skirt. Diamonds encrusted the neckline and the sleeve cuffs. An apron of white glitter cloth gave it a youthful appeal. "What about this one?"

"Seriously?" Polly stomped over to her mother. "It's so … prairie. I won't wear any dress off the rack, Mom, don't even look at them." Polly sat down on a velvet-padded bench. "What is taking Mrs. Dunkins so long?"

"What has gotten into you?" Adeline asked. "I'm trying to help."

Polly burst into tears. "Well, you're not helping."

"What's the matter? What can I do?"

"Nothing," Polly snapped. She wiped her eyes and stared out the window. "Everything is going wrong, that's all."

"Everything can't go wrong, Polly."

"Yes it can, and I don't want to talk about it," Polly argued.

Adeline knew when to leave her daughter alone. "Fine," she said.

Meanwhile, Mrs. Dunkins knew she was taking too long in the storage room, and she worried that Polly and her mother might leave to shop somewhere else. She snapped her fingers at Sasha again. "Go to the east bakery and buy one dozen of their freshest cookies. On your way back, stop at the dairy and purchase milk straight from the fattest cow. Serve Polly and her mother on my silver tray.

Hurry now! I don't want them to leave." Sasha exited out a side door and scurried off to buy the milk and cookies.

Mrs. Dunkins flipped through her fabrics at lightning speed. Princess Polly was not famous for her patience. *Oh dear, oh dear, what am I going to do?*

Mrs. Dunkins finally pulled out her best option, a bolt of light pink spidersilk. It shimmered like morning dewdrops. Sixteen thousand tiny spiders had spun the thread to make this fabric. Two thousand berries had been picked and smashed and cooked into the perfect stain to dye the cloth. A dress made of spidersilk was always beautiful and perfect for twirling.

Mrs. Dunkins shook her head and set the pink cloth back on its shelf. Polly wouldn't approve. Last year, Mrs. Dunkins had made her a yellow spidersilk dress. She knew Polly well enough to know she wouldn't wear spidersilk two years in a row.

Just then the doorbell rang, and Mrs. Dunkins gasped. *It's the new shipment*, she thought, *what good timing!* She peeked into her shop to check on Polly and Adeline. Sasha was just returning with the milk and cookies. Mrs. Dunkins ran to her service door to get the delivery from Manlaya.

"Good morning, madam," greeted the big delivery boy.

"Good morning, Tyler, do you have everything I ordered?"

"Not all of it, madam," Tyler said, looking at a piece of paper.

"Oh dear!" Mrs. Dunkins frowned.

Tyler read the packing slip. "I have three bolts of spidersilk, two bolts of satin, six spindles of lace, twenty spools of thread, ten boxes of pearls and beads, three hundred assorted buttons, eleven needles, and one bolt of mystery cloth from Lady Lily. The rest of your items will arrive in two days."

"Mystery cloth, that's great!" Lady Lily was the best designer in Manlaya and the inventor of spidersilk. She was a tiny lady and a sister to the King of Manlaya. Every now and then she sent Mrs. Dunkins a mystery cloth, a sample of her latest fabric invention. It was Mrs. Dunkins's job to make a report to Lady Lily about the cloth—if it was easy to sew and if her customers liked it or not. Mrs. Dunkins hoped the fabric inside the box would be perfect for Polly's dress.

Mrs. Dunkins paid Tyler. He left and she opened the box marked "Top Secret."

Mrs. Dunkins cut open the packaging, and light burst out of the box like shards of glass. She yelped and shut the top. *My goodness, I can't see*, she thought. Her eyes hurt from the sudden bright light. She slowly opened the box again and pulled out the fabric.

It was blinding white, and glared like sunshine on new snow. Mrs. Dunkins squinted at the cloth. Soon she noticed lovely pastel stripes—soft oranges, blues, purples, and greens shimmered across the fabric as if they were alive. Mrs. Dunkins pulled the cloth farther out of the box and gasped. "It's rainbow fabric!" she said out loud. Lady Lily had been trying to sew a rainbow into a dress since the first cloud harvest thirty years ago.

It seemed natural that a cloud and a rainbow would want to stay together, but every rainbow she sewed into a cloud dress either escaped or died within a few days. When they died, they turned black. No one in the seven kingdoms could figure out how to get the rainbows to stay alive and secure in the dresses.

Last year Lady Lily thought she had it figured out. She sent Mrs. Dunkins a beautiful cloud dress with a gorgeous rainbow woven inside by pure gold thread. Mrs. Dunkins had featured the dress in her window. The townspeople made a line all the way down Port Street to get a glimpse of it.

Of course, it was Polly who bought the dress. She put it on in the dressing room so she could wear it home. It had just stopped raining in Flores, and when Polly stepped outside the shop, the sun came out from behind the clouds. The rainbow spooked, escaped from the dress, and vanished into the sky.

Polly had been furious. Without the rainbow, it was just a plain gray cloud dress. She'd kept the dress, but had never worn it again. Polly demanded a full refund from Mrs. Dunkins and a promise that if anyone ever figured out how to make a rainbow stay in a dress, she would get the first one.

Mrs. Dunkins ran her hands over the mystery cloth, and the rainbow flickered in response to her fingertips. The cross-stitching was so intricate that Mrs. Dunkins believed the rainbow was trapped for real this time. She owed this fabric to Polly, but the mystery cloth was not soft; instead, it was as rough as the sackcloth used to bag potatoes. It would be uncomfortable to wear, and no amount of satin lining would soften it. Also, the brightness of it was annoying. As beautiful as the rainbow was, the fabric would not make a suitable dress for Polly.

Mrs. Dunkins's heart sank into her stomach. She opened the second box from Lady Lily. Inside was a pretty bolt of lavender satin. Mrs. Dunkins read the tag which explained that this particular lavender was a limited-edition color created to honor the seven kings. Only one bolt was available for dressmaking. The rest would be used to create new robes for the royal council meeting held each summer. Polly would be the only princess in the world to own this signature color. The satin fabric was signed by Lady Lily herself. Mrs. Dunkins brightened. Maybe Polly would accept it.

Mrs. Dunkins braced herself and walked back into the shop with the bolt of lavender cloth in her arms. Polly was gulping her glass of milk. "Finally," she moaned. "We ate all of the cookies!"

"I apologize, Your Highness, my order from Manlaya just arrived."

"Wonderful," the queen exclaimed, "and thank you for the cookies." Adeline elbowed her daughter in the ribs.

"Thank you for the cookies, Mrs. Dunkins," Polly repeated with a glare at her mother.

"Here is a beautiful cloth, Your Highnesses." Sasha galloped over to help Mrs. Dunkins spin the bolt and release the satin.

Mrs. Dunkins read the details about the fabric from the attached card. "This is a limited-edition cloth by Lady Lily. It is made from five hundred purple grapes, crushed and cooked along with one hundred red grapes. They steeped together for eighteen months in oak barrels. Half of the juices were bottled for the Royal Punch at the Spring Dance, and the other half were used to create this custom shade of lavender." Mrs. Dunkins draped the cloth across Polly's lap.

"The smoothest satin in Manlaya was selected and dyed with the new color." Mrs. Dunkins glanced at her packing slip. "The fabric is called the 'Lavender of Kings.' Only one bolt of this cloth is being sold this year, and I have the only bolt. I will make a dress for you, Princess Polly, and not for anyone else."

Princess Polly and her mother were silent as they stared at the cloth. "It's nice," Adeline said, but neither royal looked impressed.

Mrs. Dunkins cleared her throat. "Imagine it, Princess, you will be wearing the exact color of the royal punch."

Polly made a face. "It will look like I spilled my drink." She stamped her foot. "I don't like it, Mrs. Dunkins. Anyway, lavender is not my color."

Queen Adeline sighed. "I have to agree, Mrs. Dunkins. It's a beautiful cloth, but lavender doesn't bring out Polly's eyes. It just doesn't suit her."

Mrs. Dunkins knew they were right. She was sad. This would be the first year she didn't make Polly's dress for the Spring Dance. "I'm sorry, Princess, this is all I have for you."

Polly pointed at the storeroom. "No, I saw something through the curtain, something shiny. What do you have back there?"

"It's nothing, Your Highness, just a new cloth that isn't going to work out for a dress."

"I want to see it." Polly stood up and pushed her way through the curtain.

Mrs. Dunkins trotted after her. Polly squinted at the gleaming mystery cloth laid out on the table. "Wow, that's bright," she said. Just then the rainbow struggled, and Polly saw its shimmering colorful hues. She gasped, "It's a rainbow!" Polly clutched the fabric to her chest. "You promised this to me last year," she reminded Mrs. Dunkins. "Can the rainbow get out?"

"It's sewn in nice and tight, Princess, I don't think it can escape."

"Then I must have it. This will be my dress!" Polly frowned at Mrs. Dunkins. "Why did you keep this from me?"

Mrs. Dunkins explained. "The cloth is so rough, Your Highness. It's not going to feel good against your skin. I'm afraid it will scratch you. I was going to send it back to Lady Lily."

"I don't care if it's sandpaper," Polly growled, "I will wear that rainbow to the dance. I will be the first princess to have a *real* rainbow dress. I'm going to be on the cover of *Princess Style*, not Lexi."

Polly hugged Mrs. Dunkins hard. "You are the best." *One problem solved and one more to go,* Polly thought. Now she just needed to meet a girl with dark red hair! "Measure me, Mrs. Dunkins," Polly ordered, "we don't have all day."

Polly skipped back to the waiting area, spread her arms, and waited to be measured.

Oh dear, thought Mrs. Dunkins.

Four
~The Search~

AROUND LUNCHTIME Princess Polly and her mother left the Satin Ribbon. Sasha had measured every inch of the princess while Mrs. Dunkins selected buttons, thread, and lace for her new dress. Polly approved of the choices. The buttons were rare aqua pearls from the Azules Ocean. The lace was sky blue, and the thread was made of pure silver.

Mrs. Dunkins was one of the few dressmakers in the world who could sew with silver thread. The rainbow dress would be the loveliest at the dance, Polly was sure of it. The cloth was scratchy, but she didn't care. At least she would have a dress better than Princess Lexi's.

The princess and the queen left the dress shop in high spirits. They stopped at a few more shops on their way to lunch at the Seaside. First stop—shoes! Polly knew exactly which ones to buy. "I want the glass slippers," she told the saleslady as they entered the small store.

The glass slippers were kept in a special case. They were the most expensive shoes in all of the seven kingdoms. Even Polly had never owned a pair. Glass slippers were easily broken and not comfortable to wear, but that didn't concern Polly. They would reflect the colors in her new rainbow dress—they were perfect.

Adeline shook her head as Polly tried them on. "Those shoes are not good for dancing," she warned.

Polly rolled her eyes. "They're fine, Mama." Of the three pairs of slippers in the case, one pair fit. "I'll take them!" Polly said.

She left the store while Queen Adeline paid. The queen arranged for the shoes to be sent to their castle and then chased after her daughter. "Wait, Polly!"

Polly was already entering Tips and Tops, the glove-and-hat shop next door. Polly chose two sets of gloves and three separate hats. One set of gloves was short and blue, like the lace on her dress. The second set was long and yellow. "I don't think yellow matches your dress, Polly," Adeline pointed out.

Polly rolled her eyes. "Mother, it's a rainbow dress, I should be able to wear any color with it."

"Yes, but you've chosen blue lace to decorate the fabric. I like the blue gloves."

"Well, I can't decide, so I'm getting both pairs. I'll also take these three hats." Polly batted her long lashes. "Please, Mama."

Adeline could not say no to her only child. She was a rare queen who had not been born to a royal family. Her father was a fisherman and her mother worked at a dairy. They had seven children, and Adeline was the youngest girl.

All of Adeline's clothes were handed down to her by her older sisters. She'd never owned anything new in her life. She'd spent her childhood cleaning fish and taking care of her baby brother.

One day when King Jamie was still a prince, he fell off his pony on the beach near Adeline's home. She'd found him there, and they fell in love at first sight. Five years later, after Jamie was crowned King of Amerok, he went back to Adeline's village and married her.

Adeline and Jamie were only able to have one child, Polly. Instead of raising Polly as she'd been raised, Adeline spoiled her. Her parents might have bought Adeline new clothes if they'd been able to, but it just wasn't possible. It was possible for Adeline to spoil Polly, so she did.

"We'll take both pairs of gloves and all three hats," Queen Adeline told the shopkeeper.

"Thank you, Mom," Polly said, meaning it. She adored her mother as much as her mother adored her. Holding hands, the two royals left the shop and headed for the docks.

The Seaside restaurant was famous for its views of the Borgan Sea. It was lunchtime in Flores, and the restaurant was crowded. Polly and Adeline did not have reservations. A long line of townsfolk were waiting to be seated. A hush came over the crowd when Polly and Adeline entered the waiting area. Polly fluffed her curls.

The royals were spotted immediately by the restaurant host. He left his podium to greet them. "Good afternoon, Highnesses." He bowed. "Isn't it a lovely day?"

The royal ladies smiled at him. "It is lovely," answered Adeline. "We are exhausted from shopping."

The host nodded. "I understand. I will seat you right away, please follow me." The tall, thin man led them to a table by the window.

Polly and her mother walked by children who had been waiting in line for a long time. The children stared up at their parents. They knew cutting was not allowed, but their parents just shrugged. Polly and Adeline were royal, and certain tables were set aside only for royalty. They did not have to wait in line.

"Does this table please you, Your Highnesses?"

"Yes," answered Polly. "Water, please."

"Right away, Princess." The host bowed again and walked away.

Adeline and Polly enjoyed their lunch. The view from their table was fabulous. The Borgan Sea was emerald green in the afternoon sun. Polly could see dozens of sea turtles swimming through the clear water. In the distance a pod of dolphins played in the wake of a sailing ship. Her excitement over the rainbow dress was already wearing off. Polly fretted about Mirabel.

"Just because Mirabel has the pox doesn't mean she can't dance," Polly said, half to herself.

"Polly!" Adeline was shocked. "Your friend is very sick. She has to stay home for the next two weeks. She could get everyone else sick too! That would spoil all the summer parties back home."

Polly's shoulders sagged. "I just don't know what to do."

"You have lots of friends who can dance, sweetheart," said Adeline, patting Polly's hand.

"None with red hair."

Adeline shook her head. "I don't understand why she has to have red hair."

Polly shrugged. "If she doesn't, it just ruins everything. The different colors are part of my dance—I need one of each."

"You are a collector," said Adeline, "just like your grandfather." Polly's grandfather on her father's side had the largest collection of swords in the world. Adeline continued, "You have to have one of everything, just like he did, and you see no point in having two of the same thing."

"I am like him," Polly agreed. Her grandfather had spent his life collecting swords. He searched the whole world for what he wanted. He found exotic swords in old castles, deserted farmhouses, and tiny shops— even in the homes of regular townsfolk.

"That's it!" Polly squealed. A few non-royals glanced at their table. "I will find a regular girl, a town girl. I don't need Princess Katie after all."

"What are you talking about, Polly?"

"Pay the bill, Mother, we have more shopping to do!" They left the restaurant. "We'll begin at the Country Day School."

"What about our ice cream, Polly?" They always went to the Snow Globe after having lunch in town. "And what are we looking for at the school?"

"Forget the ice cream, Mama! I'm looking for a red-haired town girl to be in my dance. Weren't you listening?"

Adeline shrugged. "Town girls don't attend the Spring Dance, dear."

"This year, one will," Polly said. "I'll bring her as my guest, and I'll pay for her ticket with my allowance."

Adeline rolled her eyes. Polly spent all of her allowance last month on magic pixie dust, which didn't work. Adeline knew that if Polly found a town girl, she and her husband would end up buying the ticket. Adeline said nothing about this, however.

It's sweet she wants to invite a town girl, she thought. *It might be good for Polly to see how regular people live.* While Adeline didn't regret spoiling Polly, she knew her daughter didn't understand the real world. She couldn't relate to normal girls at all, and maybe it was time she tried.

Adeline and Polly hired a rickshaw to take them to the school. A rickshaw was like a horse carriage except that it was pulled by men instead of horses. Many rickshaws waited outside the restaurant to carry people around Flores. It was quicker to hire a ride than to wait for the mares to be saddled. The mares were still resting in their box stalls at the town stable.

Polly and her mother climbed into a large purple rickshaw with a velvet-padded seat. Like their lunch table, it was reserved for royals only. "To Country Day School," commanded Adeline to the rickshaw driver. He nodded and pushed off up the hill.

They followed Beach Street along the rocky coast. As they climbed the hill, the cliffs developed on the left side of the rickshaw. Country Day was located at the top, and the school did not hold their spring break at the same time as the royal schools.

The parents in Flores needed to work while the royals were in town, so Country Day stayed open. Also, the streets and shops were already overwhelmed with bored children, and the town didn't need more of them milling about.

Upon their arrival, Adeline and Polly asked their driver to wait. They exited the rickshaw and walked to the playground because it was recess time.

Country Day School was a lovely red barn that had been converted into classrooms for kindergarten through eighth grade. After eighth grade, the smartest students left Flores on the big ships. They sailed to Cantar for high school and college. Most of these children never returned. They got jobs and started families in Cantar or other kingdoms. The children who stayed in Flores learned trades like shoeing horses, raising dairy cows, managing shops, working in the royal castles, and working on the ship docks, or they became sailors.

When the children saw Princess Polly, they ran to the playground fence where she stood. They stared at her with amazement and suspicion. Royals only attended Day School on career day (which didn't make sense since becoming a royal was more of a birthright than a career path).

"I like your pants," said a cute little first-grader with two missing teeth.

"I like your dress," Polly shot back, smiling. She looked over the small crowd, and she didn't see any redheads. "Are all the students here?" Polly asked them.

"Mandy is sick," said a short, scruffy boy.

"Does she have red hair?" Polly asked hopefully.

He shrugged. "Her hair is brown."

The queen spoke up. "Do any of you know a red-haired girl about her size and age?" She pointed at Polly.

A hush fell over the children. The Queen of Amerok had spoken to them. "Y-y-yes," stammered a blond student. She pointed to the well, where a child was washing mud off her shoes. She was in the shadows, but her hair looked red. All the children stared at the girl, eyes wide. They suddenly weren't sure if it was good or bad to have red hair.

"You there, with the muddy shoes, come here," Polly called.

The girl startled. She hadn't seen Polly and Adeline by the fence. She came out of the shadows toward the crowd.

"Oh no," Polly cried. The girl's hair was bright orange. Polly needed dark red. Princess Lexi already had orange hair.

"Never mind," Polly said, waving her off.

The girl halted, looking more confused. The other kids shuffled their feet, still not sure if all of this was good or bad. The princess did not look happy.

"You should give them something," Adeline suggested.

"Like what?"

"Like this." Adeline handed Polly a handful of coins.

"Do you kids want some money?" Polly asked the group.

They cheered, deciding this was good.

Polly grinned. She handed each child a bronze coin. They took their coins and ran off shouting to one another. Polly waved goodbye to the little first-grader who'd admired her breeches. Adeline and Polly climbed back in the rickshaw.

"That was fun," Polly laughed. Giving the kids gifts made her forget about her own problems for a moment.

Adeline was pleased. "Let's get the mares and go home. To the Port Street Stables," Adeline ordered the driver. Off they went, down the hill and back to Port Street.

Polly's disappointment returned. "I don't think I'll ever find a redhead."

"Do you want to look in some of the shops?" Adeline asked.

Polly shook her head. "Town girls my age don't work, Mama. They are all at school."

"I don't know what to tell you, Polly," said Adeline. "If you didn't have to have the red hair, you would have plenty of girls to choose from."

Polly ignored Adeline. Her mother just didn't understand.

Adeline frowned. The sun was beginning to set. "It's getting late, Polly. We need to go home. I will bring you back tomorrow if you like."

Polly was tired. She remembered the beautiful rainbow fabric and felt better. At least she had solved one of her problems today. "Fine, we'll come back tomorrow."

A small bug landed near Polly's arm. She smashed it with her finger. It looked more and more like she was going to have to dye Katie's limp yellow hair. Polly leaned back and closed her eyes. *Oh, why did Mirabel have to get sick?*

Five

~The Royal Pet Palace
and Day Spa~

ADELINE AND POLLY enjoyed their ride back to the town stable. Polly leaned out of the rickshaw and watched the activity on the streets. The sailors were done working for the day. Many had been sailing for weeks, and they were happy to be on land. Tired of the food on board their ships, the sailors formed lines at the bakeries, restaurants, and taverns. Their laughter carried through the early-evening air.

"Look, Mama, there's Daisy!" Polly pointed to a little girl with a bright, round face. "Pull up to that princess!"

The driver had no trouble spotting the princess in question because Daisy was wearing her crown. He stopped on the curb next to her in front of the Snow Globe ice-cream parlor. "Daisy, it's me, Polly." Princess Daisy skipped over to Polly's rickshaw. "What are you doing?" Polly asked her friend. Daisy was one of the girls in her dance. She had light brown hair, and everybody who met Daisy liked her.

Daisy licked her ice cream. "I'm here with my parents," Daisy answered. "Guess what."

"What?"

"I had a great idea today. I stopped by your castle to tell you, but you weren't home." Daisy's brown eyes sparkled. "Do you want to hear it?"

"Of course!" Polly couldn't help but smile. Daisy's excitement was catching.

"I think we should all ride our horses to the dance this year instead of taking carriages."

Polly wrinkled her brow. She couldn't imagine riding a horse in her scratchy rainbow dress. "Why?"

"Because I think it would be fun to dye our horses to match our dresses. We could all ride up together, the six of us. No one has ever done it before. We would be the talk of the dance—of the whole Spring Festival!"

Polly imagined it: six beautiful princesses, each riding a matching beautiful horse! They would amaze everyone. "It's a fantastic idea, Daisy," she agreed. Of course, there were supposed to be *seven* of them in the dance. "So, I guess you heard about Mirabel and the pox?" Polly asked her.

Daisy pouted. "Yes, I'm so sad. What are you going to do?"

"I'm working on it," Polly muttered.

"I hired Jolee to dye my horse. She's the best, you know."

"I know. I will have her dye Tiara too."

"You better get over there before they close," Daisy urged. "Their appointment books are filling up fast."

Polly couldn't stop thinking of how great she and Tiara would look riding to the dance together. She squeezed Daisy's arm. "Tell the others," Polly said. "I want all of us to do it."

"I will," promised Daisy.

"Can we please go to one more place, Mama?" begged Polly. "I want to make an appointment for Tiara right now."

Adeline knew when to pick her battles with Polly. Right now, she was too tired to argue. "Fine," she said in defeat. "Do you want to go to the Pampered Pet or the Royal Pet Palace? I have a coupon for the Pampered Pet." Adeline dug into her purse for the coupon.

"No, we have to go to the Royal Pet Palace, Mom. I want Jolee!"

"Of course." At least the Pet Palace was on their way home. Adeline asked the driver to rush them to the Royal Pet Palace and Day

Spa. He waited outside as they entered the large brick building.

Mia almost fell over herself to greet them. "How may I help Your Highnesses?" she asked with a bow.

"I need to make an appointment for my horse and for my dog." Polly decided on the spot to dye Leroy too.

"Please follow me to the consulting room," Mia said. "Jolee will meet you there. May I offer Your Highnesses some coffee or tea while you wait?"

"She'll have tea, I'll have coffee," answered the queen. They followed Mia into a glass waiting room, where they sat in soft chairs and relaxed. Mia quickly brewed the tea and coffee. She served the royals their drinks in pet-shaped cups. Polly drank from a cat cup and Adeline drank from an elephant cup.

The royals sipped their drinks and waited for Jolee. It was nice to sit down. Presently, Jolee entered the waiting area. She was a tall girl with bright pink hair, and she wore silver sparkle eye shadow. She had five earrings in one ear, two in the other, and a diamond stud in her nose. Adeline tried not to stare.

Jolee opened her notebook. "How can I help you today, Princess?" she asked Polly.

"I need to set an appointment to have Leroy and Tiara painted for the dance."

Jolee hid her frown. The last time she worked on Tiara, the mare had tried to bite her. Jolee's boss would not allow her to say no to Polly though. She bit her tongue. "What do you have in mind?"

Polly described her dress and how she wanted Tiara and Leroy to look. "Tiara will have shimmering rainbows all over her. Please use extra glitter. I want her mane and tail braided in sky-blue ribbons the color of this bit of lace." She handed a sample of lace to Jolee. "I want Leroy's fur dyed the same blue color, and I want a big white bow on his head. When should I bring them in?" Polly was all business.

Jolee would need a lot of time. Rainbows were hard to paint, especially on a horse as wild as Tiara. "I will need three days with the horse and one with the dog," she said. Jolee wrote the appointments down on a purple card. She handed the card to Adeline.

Polly leaned toward Jolee. "Don't tell anyone about my dress," she whispered.

Jolee looked at Polly. The blue eyes of the princess darkened. "Of course not, Your Highness," Jolee promised. She closed her notebook and left the room. "Princesses," she groaned, "it's going to be a long two weeks before the dance!"

Adeline asked Mia to send for the horses. She was in no mood to wait for them at the hot stable, and her feet hurt. The queen and her daughter went outside to dismiss the rickshaw driver. Adeline thanked him with a large tip.

Meanwhile, Cianna was upstairs cleaning her washing room. She'd ended up washing eight pets after Trixi, and now her back hurt from all the hours she'd spent bent over her washtub. She loved her job, but it was very tiring, especially for a fourteen-year-old girl. Sometimes she wished she were back at school with the other kids.

Of course, Cianna missed her parents too—even though her mom had died soon after she was born. Her father's favorite stories were about how much Cianna resembled her mother, Emma. It had not been easy for Tristan to raise a blind girl by himself, but he'd enjoyed every minute with his daughter.

Tristan had quit sailing after her mother died and had taken a job at the town stable. Cianna had spent most of her afternoons there learning about horses. Cianna loved horses, but her father wouldn't permit her to ride them.

When Cianna was eight, the captain of the *Majestic* offered Tristan a job on his ship. An illness had taken over most of the ship's sailors. The captain needed help for a short trip to Sandia and back to pick up the sugar harvest. Her father was offered a lot of money for this journey because it was on short notice. Tristan arranged for Cianna's babysitter, Mia, to watch her while he was away.

Cianna remembered waving to her father when he sailed away. She couldn't see him, but she could smell the salt of the sea and hear the creaking of the *Majestic*. She had not let herself cry. After all, he would return. But he never did.

No one knows what happened to the *Majestic* that summer. It did not reach its destination in Sandia, and it never returned to Flores. Rescue ships searched for twenty-one days, but there was no sign of the *Majestic* or Cianna's father. The sugar crop rotted on the docks in Sandia. It was the worst summer of Cianna's life. And because of the sugar shortage, there were few sweets in Flores that year.

Cianna missed her father. At night he used to toss her into her bed as she squealed with laughter. He taught her how to find her way around Flores without asking for help. He taught her to use her ears, nose, and hands to "see" the world around her. He made a cane for her out of the heart of an oak tree, and he taught her to be happy, grateful, hard-working, and punctual.

Cianna knew she amazed everyone she met. She could smell food and know exactly what it was. She could hear footsteps and know the mood of the person who was coming (and if they needed a bath)! She was pleasant and brave, and she was never late. She owed it all to her father, and she would never stop missing him.

Mia ran upstairs to talk to Cianna. "Guess who just left."

"Who?"

"Princess Polly and Queen Adeline!" Mia gushed. She was crazy about the royals. "I wish you could see her, Cianna. Princess Polly is so beautiful! She was wearing the cutest riding outfit."

"Why was she here?" Cianna wondered which of Polly's animals she'd be washing soon.

"She's having Leroy and Tiara painted for the Spring Dance."

Cianna giggled. "I bet Jolee isn't happy about that." Cianna knew how crazy Tiara could be. She had bathed the mare many times.

"Which perfume was the princess wearing?" Cianna asked.

"I don't know!" Mia said.

Cianna didn't understand how people could miss such important details.

"Take me to where she was; I bet I will still be able to tell. First, let me lock up." Cianna locked her washing room. After two years of working at the Pet Palace, it was her second home. She and Mia skipped down to the glass consulting room.

Royals wore the loveliest perfumes in Windym. Cianna had memorized the scent of every fragrance created since she'd moved in above the perfume shop. She took a big whiff of the odors in the consulting room. She smiled. "It's faint now, but Polly is wearing Unicornia," Cianna said. "It's a new perfume, just invented. It's going to be popular this summer."

"Especially with Polly wearing it," Mia agreed. "Oh my goodness," she gasped, "the princess left her riding gloves." Mia lifted the gloves off the chair. Her stomach dropped. Would she be blamed for the gloves being left behind? "Maybe the princess is still outside."

Just then Polly walked back into the Pet Palace looking for her gloves. Polly glimpsed the two friends through the glass wall, and her mouth fell open when she saw Cianna's dark red hair.

Mia noticed the princess staring at them. *Oh no*, thought Mia, *she sees me holding the gloves.*

She thinks I stole them. Mia bit her lip. "The princess is back," she said to Cianna. The two girls walked out of the glass room.

Polly rushed toward them.

"I'm so sorry, Your Highness, I just found them," Mia stammered. She bowed and held out the gloves.

Polly brushed past the receptionist and stood face-to-face with Cianna. "Your hair," she said to Cianna, "it's red."

Cianna froze as the princess twirled the long strands in her fingers. *What is going on*, wondered Cianna.

"It's the perfect shade of red," Polly noted. She measured herself against Cianna. "You're older than I am, but we're about the same size." She grabbed the pet washer's chin and moved her face from side to side. "You're pretty too. Can you dance?"

Cianna's father had taught her to dance. "Yes," Cianna fumbled. She wondered what this was about. No stranger, let alone a royal, had ever paid her so much attention.

"That's wonderful." Polly decided Cianna was a good choice to take Mirabel's place in *The Seven Sisters*. "And your eyes are the same color as the Borgan Sea! I was just looking at it during lunch." Polly was delighted. "You are perfect."

Mia watched all this in amazement, still holding the gloves. She spoke up for her friend. "Her name is Cianna," Mia said, wondering what the princess wanted with her. "She's blind."

"You mean she can't see?" Polly was horrified.

"Right," said Mia.

Cianna couldn't see with her eyes, but the rich smells coming off Polly spoke volumes. The princess smelled like horse sweat, chocolate pudding, Unicornia perfume, lavender shampoo, and scented nail polish— all at once.

"Well, I'm sorry you're blind," Polly said to Cianna.

"It's okay, I'm used to it."

"How do you get around?" the princess asked.

"Very well," Cianna answered, gripping the cane she rarely used, "better than most people." Cianna smiled to herself. She often heard the citizens of Flores tripping over their own feet or stumbling into holes—and they could see!

"I like your spirit," laughed Polly. "Let's be friends."

Cianna could not see Polly's fancy clothes, her pampered skin, her expensive hairstyle, her diamond earrings, or her new boots, but she liked her sweet, friendly voice. *She's a girl like me*, Cianna thought. "I'd love to be friends."

"Great!" Polly shook her hand and the two girls giggled.

Mia almost passed out. "Here are your gloves," she said, giving them to Polly.

"Why thank you, miss. I'm so happy I came back for these." Polly looked at Cianna. "Will you come to my castle for dinner this evening?"

Cianna was stunned. She'd never been to anyone's home except for Mia's and Mr. Talley's (for his annual employee party). Cianna had nothing to do today, she'd already locked up her washing room, and there was no reason she couldn't leave with Polly. *It will be an adventure*, she decided. "I would like that."

"Perfect," Polly said. "My mare, Tiara, is outside; we'll ride her double."

Not Tiara, she thought. "Take care of this for me," Cianna said to Mia. She handed over her smooth wooden cane.

"Are you sure?" Mia asked.

"I'm sure! I don't want it banging on the horse and scaring her, and you know I don't need it."

Mia snorted. "That's for sure." Mia was one of the people who were constantly tripping. Still in a daze, Mia took the cane and waved goodbye to her blind friend. Cianna sensed the movement and waved back. She knew Mia would expect to hear every detail about her adventure tomorrow.

Cianna and Polly left the Pet Palace together. "There's Tiara," Polly said. "Isn't she beautiful?" Polly had already forgotten Cianna was blind. "And this is my mother." She pointed at Adeline. "Mother, this is Cianna. She's my new friend." Polly glanced at Cianna, who was looking at nothing. "Oh yeah," Polly remembered aloud, "she's blind."

Adeline noticed Cianna's red hair. She sighed. *Polly found her dancer—but a blind girl?* Adeline didn't see how this was going to work. She looked like a sweet child. She had a sad angel face and the greenest eyes. "It's a pleasure to meet you, Cianna," Adeline said.

Cianna liked the regal queen's voice; it melted off her tongue like warm butter. "I am pleased to meet you, Your Highness."

"She's coming to dinner, Mother," Polly announced. "Can we have a sleepover?"

Cianna had never been invited to a sleepover. Her heart thrummed with excitement. She faced the queen, thinking, *Please say yes.*

"Is it okay with her parents?"

"I don't have parents, Your Highness, I'm an orphan."

The queen sucked in her breath. *A blind, beautiful, sweet orphan!* Why, she was ready to hand Cianna the keys to her castle. "Then it's settled, you're having a sleepover."

Polly grabbed Cianna's hands and the girls squealed, jumping up and down. Cianna had no idea, until this moment, how much she missed the girls at school. Even though she hadn't been able to do her lessons, she'd enjoyed the other kids. How she missed having friends!

The stable boy who brought the horses to the Pet Palace helped Cianna and Polly mount Tiara, who was in a great mood. She'd enjoyed a nice rubdown at the stable. For lunch she'd been fed a hot bran mash drizzled with molasses and served with a side of baby carrots. Also, the mare remembered Cianna as the nice girl who sometimes gave her a bath. Tiara didn't make a fuss when both girls climbed on her back.

Cianna loved horses, and she'd ridden double before with her father, he had allowed her to do that, but her dream was to ride a horse by herself someday.

"Let's go home," Polly said.

They trotted down Port Street. The sailors and shoppers all stopped to stare. The fancy royals on their fancy horses were exciting, but it was the little girl in shabby clothes riding with Polly who caught their attention. *What was the prettiest princess in the seven kingdoms doing with the poorest girl in Flores?*

By the time Tiara trotted through the town gates, the news had spread from the Snow Globe to the docks. Everyone was curious about the unusual friendship between the princess and the pet washer.

Cianna didn't know how drab she looked sitting behind Polly. She was thrilled because she'd met a fun girl her age—a girl who smelled wonderful, had a sweet mother, and owned a lot of pets. Cianna was happy. She was going to have her first sleepover!

Six

~The Sleepover~

"WE'RE HERE," yelled Polly. The group rode right up to the massive front door of the castle. Caden had seen them coming, and he was waiting to take the horses. The kennel dogs heard the approaching hoofbeats and a chorus of barking echoed across the green valley.

"How many dogs do you have, Polly?" Cianna asked.

"I've lost count. The dogs live in the kennel behind the stable, and I have one in every color and every size."

"I've only met Leroy."

"He's my favorite," Polly explained. "He's the prettiest." The pride in Polly's voice was obvious, but Cianna felt bad for all the dogs that stayed locked in the kennel.

The breeze shifted, carrying a sweet scent. "You have a lot of roses too," Cianna said as they dismounted.

"How do you know that?" marveled Polly.

Cianna smiled. "I can smell them. You must have a million of them."

Polly looked around. She did have thousands of roses. Mini-roses, large roses, rose trees, rose shrubs, rose vines—roses in every color of course. She had been crazy for roses when she was five years old. Her father had planted them in front of the castle for her birthday. With new eyes, she saw her father's gift. "I guess I do have a lot of roses," she agreed. "I don't really notice them anymore, but I wish you could see them."

Cianna shrugged. "My father used to have a saying: 'Nothing looks as good as it smells.'"

Polly closed her eyes and sniffed the air. "They make me feel good inside," she said. "They smell like—"

"They smell like love," finished Cianna.

Polly opened her eyes. "Yes, like love." Polly gave the reins to Caden. "Tiara was a good girl on the way home," she boasted to him.

"Yes, Your Highness." Caden bowed to hide his smirk. He was astonished that Polly had made friends with a poor town girl, and he couldn't help but notice Cianna's beautiful, slightly sad face. She looked delicate, breakable even.

Caden lived in an apartment above the stable. He went to town often for the king and queen, to see his friends who worked in Flores, or to visit his uncle. He'd never seen this red-haired girl before. It was obvious she didn't work for a royal family because castle workers dressed in fancy uniforms.

He looked at Cianna's hands. Her nails were short and her skin was rough and dry. *She probably washes dishes*, he thought, although she looked too young to be working at all.

"Caden, the horses," Polly snapped.

"Yes, Your Highness." Caden bowed. "Good evening, ladies." He led Mina and Tiara away.

He seems like a nice boy, Cianna thought. His voice was strong and calm. She'd noticed the horses nickering quiet greetings to him. If horses liked him, he had to be a kind person. Animals always knew best.

"Take my arm, Cianna, and let's go inside," said Polly.

Queen Adeline followed the girls into the castle.

King Jamie was back from hunting. He stood in the entryway and gave his wife and daughter a huge hug when they walked in. "And who is this young lady?" he asked.

"This is Cianna. She works at the Pet Palace and she's blind," Polly said.

The king didn't miss a beat. "Welcome, Cianna, my castle is your castle." He gave her arm a gentle squeeze.

Cianna sensed that he was a very large man. He had a booming voice and thick fingers. He was cheerful, which reminded Cianna of her father. She liked him already.

"Were you hunting wild boar today, Your Highness?" Cianna asked the king.

"Yes, how did you know?"

"It's the mud you used to hide your scent, my dad used the same kind when he went hunting. I also smell blood, not yours I hope?"

He chuckled. "You're a clever girl, Cianna. Yes, the blood is mine. I cut my hand climbing a fence."

"Let me see that wound," said the queen. She grabbed her husband's hand and led him away. "Dinner is at seven, girls!" she called over her shoulder.

"Hey, no yelling in the castle," shouted Polly. That started a giggling fit with Cianna. "Let me show you … I mean, take you to my room."

Polly held Cianna's hand. They walked up twenty-two stairs. They turned left and walked sixty steps, until Polly stopped and said they had arrived. They went inside her room and Polly shut the door.

Cianna's feet sank into thick carpet. "What's your room like?"

Polly looked around. "Well, it's big. I have a canopy bed, a walk-in closet, two dressers, three toy chests, one bookcase, and one stage for putting on small shows. There's also a bathroom, a sitting area, a vanity table, a desk, and a window seat." Polly sighed. "It's a lot to clean."

Cianna sniffed the air. "Is Leroy here?"

"Yes!" exclaimed Polly, amazed again by her new friend. "He's lazy. I bet he hasn't left the window seat since this morning."

Cianna stepped carefully through the room toward the smell of the perfumed dog. She sat next to him and stroked his back. Leroy rolled over for a tummy rub and wagged his tail. He remembered Cianna too.

"It's funny how you already know my pets, Cianna, even though we've never met before."

"I know all the royal pets."

The two girls sat with Leroy and gossiped about the pets from all the different castles. They talked about their hair, their skin conditions, and their bad breath. Cianna knew all about the animals, and Polly knew all about the owners, and the girls enjoyed trading information. The more Cianna learned about the owners, the more she understood the pets.

Soon they were called to dinner. "I have to put Leroy out first," said Polly. Cianna heard the window open, a bunch of weird noises, and then Leroy barked, sounding far away.

"What did you just do?" she asked.

"Oh, I keep forgetting you can't see," Polly said. "Leroy is lazy. He doesn't like to walk up and down the stairs. I have this pulley system for him. I put him in the basket and then lower him to the ground. Now he's off playing. When he's done, he'll get back in the basket and sleep until I pull him back up."

"Wow, he is lazy!" Cianna agreed. The two girls laughed.

"It's seven, let's go." Polly led Cianna down the stairs and through the large castle. Their footsteps echoed on the marble floors, and Cianna sensed the ceilings were high and vaulted. Soon they entered the dining room. Cianna sat next to Polly at a wooden table. The king and queen were already there.

The king spoke first. "Since I didn't get my boar today, we'll be having chicken this evening, Cianna."

"I love chicken, sir," Cianna said. "Everything smells so good—the sweet potatoes, the garlic green beans, the vegetable soup, and the avocado salad!" Cianna was starving.

The king grinned. "You are amazing, my girl! You guessed right on everything."

I didn't guess, corrected Cianna in her mind. "I also smell lemon candles burning on the table, and there is a dog sitting next to you, not Leroy. There is an apple pie cooking in the kitchen, and fresh tulips are on the table." Cianna grinned. She was showing off, just a little.

The king, queen, and Polly clapped their hands. "I think you see the world better than most people," Adeline commented. The kitchen workers served the dinner and the four of them had a nice time eating and talking.

Later, they went to the back patio for their pie. The large dog who had been sitting next to the king trotted outside with them. His name was Hunter. He needed a bath and a tooth brushing, but Cianna didn't think it would be polite to mention that.

After dinner and dessert, the two girls said good night to the king and queen. They returned to Polly's room for their evening baths.

"I really like your parents," Cianna said.

Polly shrugged. "They're okay."

The girls filled the bath with water and bubbles. Cianna could have washed three large dogs in Polly's tub. The girls splashed water all over the bathroom and pretended they were mermaids in the ocean. They blew bubbles, made soap beards, and played with toy boats and dolphins.

When it was over, Polly let Cianna borrow a flowercloth nightgown. As Cianna pulled it over her head, she smelled sweet jasmine. Cianna slid her hands down the borrowed gown. She had never worn anything so soft.

Polly noticed Cianna's attention to the material. "Your gown is purple," she said. "I have those nightgowns in every color. I also have slippers in every color and bathrobes in every color." Polly brushed her thick black hair.

"You're lucky," marveled Cianna, "I've never seen a color."

Polly gasped. "You've never seen a color!"

Cianna shrugged. "I was born blind, so I never have."

"How do you know if something is pretty or not?"

"I don't," said Cianna. "I don't even think about it."

Polly could not imagine what she would do if she couldn't see. "How do you pick your clothes? How do you pick your friends?"

Cianna giggled. "I don't understand how my eyes could help me choose a friend!" She braided her thick hair as she spoke. "I don't know if you're pretty or not; I just like you for who you are. And I think you're fun," she added.

"I'm fun?"

"Yes, and you have a nice family."

"I guess so," Polly said. "Oops, I forgot Leroy!" Polly ran to the window and looked down. Leroy was waiting in his basket. He whined when he saw her. "I'm sorry," Polly called to him, pulling the basket up. "I always forget Leroy," she confessed.

Polly took Leroy out of the basket and shut the window. She climbed into her tall bed and pulled Cianna up too. "Let's go to sleep; we have a lot to do tomorrow." Polly looked at Cianna's beautiful dark red hair. She still couldn't believe her luck. Tomorrow she would start teaching Cianna the dance. Polly liked Cianna. She would miss her once the dance was over.

"Yes, let's sleep," Cianna agreed. "I'm going to be busy at work tomorrow."

"What?" Polly cried. She sat up in her bed. "I want you to stay with me."

"I wish I could, but we're so busy right now. I have to go to work. Also, I have to earn money to pay my rent."

Polly fretted. She needed Cianna for the dance. She would have to convince her. "I really want you to stay with me," Polly said. She made her best begging face, the one that worked on her mother. But Cianna didn't notice. *Ughhh*, Polly remembered, *she's blind*.

"I can't stay with you," Cianna repeated. "I want to, but I can't." Cianna was sad. Other than Mia, she had no friends.

"Can you come back after work?" Polly asked.

Cianna brightened. "I can do that."

Polly clapped her hands. "Great! I will have Caden pick you up in our carriage tomorrow afternoon."

"Really?" Cianna had never ridden in a carriage.

"Sure," Polly said. "In fact, I'll also have him drive you to work in the morning."

Polly turned out the lights, and the room went black. "Oh no," Polly gasped, "my glow bugs must have died. I can't see anything!"

"Neither can I!" Cianna exclaimed, pretending to be scared.

Polly paused. "But—" Then she laughed, delighted with Cianna's joke. Polly lit the scented candle next to her bed and the smell of warm vanilla filled the room.

Cianna and Polly whispered stories to each other. Leroy jumped into the bed and snuggled between them. Before long, the three of them were fast asleep.

Seven

~Cianna Smells a Rat~

THE NEXT MORNING Polly and Cianna enjoyed breakfast on the patio. Polly informed her mother Cianna would be coming over every day after work, and the queen was pleased. She and her husband admired the polite and hard-working girl.

"I'm going to have Caden drive her into Flores this morning, Mother," Polly said.

"Wonderful! I will join you for the ride, Cianna. It's my turn to choose a dress." Adeline winked at Polly.

"Good luck, Mama, because the best dress in town is already taken," Polly said.

"That may be so, little one, but my days of being the belle of the ball are over. I just want something nice and comfortable. I'm sure Mrs. Dunkins will have the perfect fabric for me."

"Don't get too comfortable," snorted Polly. "You still need to look pretty. You are the Queen of Amerok after all."

Cianna listened to the mother-daughter conversation with curiosity. Her own mother, Emma, had held her for just a moment, and then never again. Cianna couldn't remember that moment, though she cherished it with all her heart. She imagined her mother hugging her and singing to her. Next to that, she knew nothing about mothers.

Polly teased Adeline a lot, but Cianna felt how much they loved each other. What concerned her was all their talk about how pretty things were, or weren't. *Was this normal for people who could see?* Her father and Mia had taught her that looks didn't matter—to judge objects by their quality of workmanship, and to judge people by how they treated her. Cianna was worried. Maybe how she looked was more important than she realized.

The chirping of bluebirds interrupted her thoughts and Cianna knew it was almost time for work. "I need to go," she said.

"Of course!" Adeline jumped out of her chair. "You can't be late. I'm sure the carriage is ready. Goodbye, my sweet." Cianna heard Adeline kiss Polly.

"Goodbye, Polly," said Cianna. "I'll see you tonight."

"Great," Polly said. "I'm going to see the other princesses today at the jousting tournament. I can't wait to tell them about you! You'll meet them after work."

Cianna hoped they would like her. "Don't forget you're out of glow bugs," she reminded the princess.

"Right! I will start hunting for new ones right now."

The girls giggled, remembering all the fun they'd had during the sleepover. Cianna followed Adeline through the castle, counting their footsteps. They walked for so long she lost track of them. Finally, they arrived at the front door. Cianna knew where they were because she could smell the rose bushes again.

"Good morning, Your Highness," said a familiar voice. It was the stable boy, Caden.

"Good morning, Caden," replied Adeline. "We're going to Flores, and please hurry. I don't want Cianna to be late for work."

"Yes, Your Highness. Where am I taking her?"

"To the Royal Pet Palace and Day Spa," announced the queen.

Cianna heard Adeline enter the carriage. Then a warm hand touched her arm. "May I help you inside, miss?" Caden asked, his voice was deep and gentle.

She nodded and Caden easily lifted her into the carriage. The carriage rocked as he took his place in the driver's seat.

Caden gathered the reins. As small as Cianna was, he sensed her strength. She let him help her into the carriage, but he knew she could have climbed in herself. Cianna was a refreshing change from Polly, and Caden enjoyed having a non-royal person around. He clucked to the horses. They pulled away from the castle and trotted to Flores.

Caden parked in front of the Pet Palace and opened the carriage door. Before he could help Cianna out, Mia came barreling out of the spa with a huge grin on her face. She dragged Cianna out of the carriage and thanked the queen for bringing her back.

"You're welcome," Adeline said. "Take me to Bun Buns, Caden, I'm craving a scone."

Caden took his seat and steered the horses to Bun Buns.

Mia watched the carriage pull away then turned to Cianna. "You have to tell me all about it!"

Cianna frowned. The town bell rang at least ten minutes ago. She was late for work, and she'd never been late for work before.

"What's wrong?" asked Mia. "Didn't you have a good time?"

"Oh yes, and I will tell you all about it, but I think I have ten pets to wash today and I'm already behind."

They went inside and Mia checked her books. "Actually, you have thirteen pets to wash, and the first one is already upstairs waiting for you." Mia squealed and hugged her friend. "Let's talk at lunch. I have a *million* questions!"

Cianna smiled. "Deal."

Cianna spent the day washing animals. She washed three birds, two cats, one fox, two monkeys, one dog, one baby elephant, one small black bear, one jackrabbit, and one horse. She had a nice lunch with Mia in the middle of the day and told her all about her sleepover with Princess Polly. Cianna was getting ready to leave work when one last pet came in to be washed.

Mia and the owner brought the animal upstairs to Cianna's washroom. "This is Princess Anna," said Mia.

Cianna smelled a pet rat and a princess who was wearing too much perfume. "It's a pleasure to meet you, Princess." Cianna held out her hand. It was unusual for an owner to come up to the washing room. The princess shook her hand with ice-cold fingers.

"This is my rat," said the princess in a high voice. "His name is Peaches. You can leave us," she ordered Mia.

Cianna heard Mia leave the room.

"I'm having a tea party tomorrow afternoon," Princess Anna explained. "Peaches is going to perform for my friends. He's trained to ride a bike, walk a tightrope, and draw pictures on a chalkboard. He is no ordinary rat." Cianna heard the pride in Anna's voice. "I need you to wash him. He's been burrowing in the garden again, and I would prefer he smelled like flowers, not dirt."

"Of course, Your Highness, I will start right now." Cianna was supposed to be off work and on her way to Polly's. *Well, it doesn't take long to wash a rat*, she thought.

Princess Anna walked to the tub. Cianna heard her moving the wash bottles around, and Cianna didn't like that. "The bottles are made of glass, Princess Anna. If you bump them, they could break and someone might get hurt." *That someone would probably be me*, thought Cianna.

Anna walked back over to her. "Well, here he is then," Princess Anna said. She plopped the rat in Cianna's hands. "Please hurry, he's having his nails painted next. I'll wait here for him."

Cianna did not mind rushing. She was looking forward to playing with Polly again. She reached for her soap bottle, and it took her a moment to find it. Anna must have moved the bottle.

Cianna used the same shampoo on the majority of the pets. The conditioners were different. Each one had special ingredients to treat the skin, the flea, or the hair conditions of each animal. She kept the conditioners in a cupboard. She marked each of them with scratches on the glass that she could trace with her fingertips. Each type of conditioner had a different set of scratches. It was how Cianna kept track of them.

She began washing Peaches. He was a sweet rat. He didn't squirm or try to bite, but the shampoo felt slimy and smelled odd. Cianna made a mental note to make a new batch in the morning.

She finished scrubbing the rat and rinsed off the lather. The odd odor filled the room, and then Cianna felt hair coming off of Peaches. *That's strange*, she thought. She didn't remember rats shedding their hair in the spring. She rubbed Peaches as she rinsed him. More and more hair was coming off! Cianna's heart dropped into her stomach. Something was wrong.

Then Cianna heard footsteps. Anna walked to the tub and sobbed. "Peaches! Oh, Peaches! What have you done to him?"

Cianna turned the water off and dried Peaches. She couldn't see how bad it was. After she dried him, Cianna rubbed her hands over the rat and sucked in her breath. There wasn't a hair left on the poor animal, and Peaches was shivering.

Cianna felt Anna grab the rat from her. "Look what you did," she cried. "He's bald!" Anna sobbed so loudly that other Pet Palace workers began to gather around the washroom.

"What happened?" It was the owner of the spa, Mr. Talley. He was out of breath from running up the stairs.

"Look what she did to Peaches!" Cianna imagined Anna holding the hairless rat in his face.

"Cianna, can you explain this?" Mr. Talley was horrified.

Cianna lifted her chin. "I don't know, Mr. Talley. I washed him with my soap and all his hair fell out." Cianna was also horrified. "I don't understand it, sir. I'm so sorry, Princess Anna."

"Sorry!" the princess exclaimed. "You're sorry? Look what you did to him."

Anna shoved the rat under her nose, and Cianna smelled again the odd scent of the shampoo. It was not an ingredient she used in her soap. It was harsh, like black tar. Maybe the rat was sick. Or maybe her shampoo had gone bad in the spring heat. Whatever it was, Cianna knew better than to blame Peaches. She would have to take the blame herself.

"I am truly sorry, Your Highness." Cianna bowed her head. She felt everyone in the room staring at her.

"Can you fix him?" Anna asked.

"No, Your Highness," replied Cianna. She didn't have any medicine that would grow hair by tomorrow!

Anna took a deep breath. "I would like her suspended, Mr. Talley, for what she did to my pet."

Mr. Talley did not expect this. "W-what?" he stammered.

"Suspend her," Anna repeated. "She should be punished for what she did."

Mr. Talley didn't answer. Cianna knew what was going through his mind. It was the busiest time of year. He needed Cianna to work. She imagined him standing there with his mouth open.

"I didn't say fire her, just suspend her please, for two weeks."

"Two weeks?" he whispered.

The two busiest weeks of the year, thought Cianna. She hung her head, waiting for her fate to be decided. All the workers who had come to see what had happened tiptoed out of the room.

Princess Anna's parents owned the Port Street Pet Shop, just down the road. They were Mr. Talley's best customers. He had to make Anna happy. The naked rat was shivering in Anna's hands. Mr. Talley couldn't deny that a mistake had been made. He was lucky Anna wasn't asking him to fire Cianna.

"Yes, Princess Anna, I will suspend her for two weeks. Cianna, you may leave now."

Cianna gasped. How could this be happening to her?

"Thank you, Mr. Talley," said Anna. "Now, what are you going to do for Peaches?"

Mr. Talley and Anna walked out of the room discussing the hairless rat. Cianna heard Mr. Talley offer to buy the rodent a new set of clothing. He also offered Peaches a free massage, a heat wrap, and a pedicure.

Stunned, Cianna gathered her coat and purse. She blinked and a huge tear fell from her eye.

She locked her washroom, went downstairs, and dropped her keys on the front desk. Mia was there. She grabbed Cianna's hand and squeezed it. They couldn't speak because Anna was standing in the lobby with Mr. Talley. Cianna heard Anna laughing as Mr. Talley tried to make her happy with jokes.

Cianna swallowed the lump in her throat and dried her tears. She held her head up high and walked out of the Pet Palace. Something was wrong—she knew it. Her soap had not caused Peaches's hair to fall out. Cianna would not feel ashamed.

She stepped onto the sidewalk and a gentle hand gripped her arm. "This way, miss."

Cianna's heart skipped a beat. It was Caden. He'd come to pick her up from work. In all the mess with Peaches, she'd forgotten. She hesitated a moment.

"Are you still coming to visit Princess Polly?" he asked. Caden could tell something had upset Cianna by her bright red eyes.

Cianna thought about it. *Why not?* She had nothing better to do, and Polly would cheer her up. "Yes, I am." Cianna let herself smile, and it lit up her sad face like the sun. Caden couldn't help but admire the determined little pet washer.

"Here's the carriage." Caden guided Cianna onto a velvet seat. The carriage top was down so she could feel the warm spring breeze.

"Are we picking the queen up too?" Cianna asked.

"No, miss, I took her home at lunchtime."

"Did she find a dress?"

Caden laughed. "I have no idea, miss. Shopping isn't one of my interests." His manner was genuine and easy.

"I can't say it's one of mine either," said Cianna.

Caden clucked to the horses. They trotted onto the street and pulled the carriage out of Flores.

Cianna and Caden chatted all the way to Polly's. They talked about everything under the sun except their jobs. By the time they reached Polly's castle, they were friends.

Cianna learned they both lived without their parents. Caden was older than she by two years. His uncle had raised him because his father was a full-time sailor. When Caden took the job at Polly's, he was offered the apartment in the stable. He took it and moved out of his uncle's overcrowded home in Flores.

Caden only saw his father twice a year when his ship docked. His mother lived far away in Cantar. She moved there to finish college. Her dream was to open a saddle shop in Flores and to buy a small ranch for Caden in Windym so he could raise and train his own horses. Cianna thought it was sad that her school was so far away.

Soon they arrived back at Polly's castle, and the princess ran out the front door.

"Cianna, you're finally here!" She pulled Cianna out of the carriage. "Thanks, Caden," she said, dismissing him. Cianna heard the horses trot downhill to the stable.

"We have so much to do," Polly said.

"Oh, like what?"

"Didn't I mention my dance?" Polly asked. "I want you to be in my performance of *The Seven Sisters* at the Spring Festival in two weeks."

Cianna frowned. "No, you didn't, you know I have a job. Anyway, I don't have a ticket to the Spring Festival."

"Oh," Polly grunted, sounding disappointed.

Cianna sighed. *I guess I can help Polly out now that I'm suspended*, she thought. "Well, something did happen at work today that has given me some free time."

Polly brightened. "What happened?"

Cianna didn't want to explain about Peaches. "I got some time off is all. Actually, I have two weeks off."

"That's perfect!" cheered Polly. "After you left this morning, I went to the jousting field to watch Prince Jayson practice." Polly sighed, forgetting for a moment what she was saying. She seemed to forget herself a lot when she talked about Prince Jayson. "Anyway, my friends were there and I was telling them that I wished you didn't work so that you could practice with us. I need a dancer and you're available. It looks like I got my wish!"

"Yes, that is lucky," Cianna agreed with little enthusiasm. At least her bad news was good news for Polly.

"And don't worry about your ticket, Cianna, I'll get you one!"

"Really?" Cianna knew how expensive they were.

"Sure," Polly said, faltering. She had not only spent all of her allowance, she'd taken an advance on next month's allowance too. Maybe she could borrow money from Daisy. "Well, don't worry," she said, deciding not to think about it. "I'll get you there!"

Polly led her inside the castle. Cianna was happy she could help her new friend, and she couldn't believe she'd be going to the Spring Festival, but none of that made her less sad about her suspension.

She thought about poor naked Peaches. Something just wasn't right about it. Maybe someday she would understand, but for now she would try to enjoy her extra time with Polly.

Eight

~*The Seven Sisters*~

POLLY GUIDED CIANNA upstairs to her room. Cianna heard lots of high voices chattering with each other. The room went silent when they entered.

"She's here," Polly announced. She held Cianna's hand high as though she'd just won her in a contest. "Everyone, this is my new friend, Cianna."

"Hi, Cianna," said several voices at once.

"I will introduce you," said Polly. "Line up girls." Polly walked Cianna down the line. She introduced each princess one by one. Cianna shook all their hands. There was Princess Daisy, Princess Lexi, Princess Cidnee, Princess Laci, Princess Katie, and lastly, Princess Anna.

Princess Anna! Cianna sucked in her breath. *Was it the same Princess Anna who had just gotten her suspended?*

"Hello again," Princess Anna said. Cianna recognized the familiar movements of someone extending her hand. Cianna was polite and shook Anna's hand.

"I galloped my horse all the way here. That's how I beat you."

"Oh," said Cianna. She could think of nothing else to say. She focused on the other princesses. Daisy was friendly, Cidnee was funny, Laci and Katie were sisters and younger than the other girls—they were nice too. Lexi made it clear she was Polly's best friend, and she was not friendly. Anna, on the other hand, no longer seemed angry about Peaches.

"No worries about my rat," she said, soothing the awkwardness between them. "Mr. Talley fixed him up with a sweater vest, wool pants, and ear muffs. He looks darling. You can hardly tell he lost all his hair. I'm picking him up tomorrow after his free pedicure."

"What are you two talking about?" asked Polly.

"Nothing," Anna and Cianna said at the same time, neither of them wanted to relive the horror at the Pet Palace.

Cianna knew Mr. Talley would have a hard time without her at work. She felt sorry for him and the other workers at the spa. *Does Anna even realize what she's done?*

Cianna felt along Polly's bedroom wall until she found the window seat. She sat and the fresh air smelled good.

Princess Polly looked around her room. All of her friends were pretty except for Katie. She had dirty-blond hair, gray eyes, and was always pale. But Katie was not in the dance. She was Laci's sister, and she played the music.

Polly noticed how well Cianna fit in with the other dancers. She had thick hair down to her waist. It was bronze red with streaks of fiery gold. She had sea-green eyes and a sad but still very cute face. Only her clothes didn't look right. They were shabby and worn and the colors didn't match. Polly decided she would fix that problem by giving Cianna some of her old clothes.

Overall, Polly was satisfied with the different looks of her friends. Laci had short white-blond hair. She was Katie's sister, but she hadn't inherited her plain features. Daisy's hair was a yummy caramel color and her skin was dark brown. Anna's hair was straight and golden. Her best friend, Lexi, had shiny copper curls. Cidnee's long waves were dark brown and she had the same toast-colored skin as Daisy. Cianna's hair was the perfect shade of dark red that had been so hard to find, and Polly's black curls completed the collection. *We are going to amaze everyone,* Polly thought.

"Let's get started!" Polly clapped her hands. "We need to help Cianna catch up."

Polly grabbed Cianna's arm and led her onto the stage. "Katie, start the music."

Lovely melodies filled the air and Cianna recognized the vibrant plucking of a harp. Polly held both of Cianna's arms and pulled her around like a puppet. "One and two," counted Polly, forcing Cianna's legs to move. Cianna felt silly. Was everyone watching? She knew Polly was bossy, but this was too much!

Cianna shook her head. "Just dance next to me and tell me the steps," she said.

"Suit yourself," huffed Polly. "Okay, let's get in our places, and we'll all teach Cianna the dance."

The music halted as the princesses shuffled to their places. Polly showed Cianna where to stand.

"*The Seven Sisters* begins with three spins to the right and then three spins to the left on our toes. Make your arms into a circle. Then we sashay forward six steps and curtsey, then we dip and twirl." Polly went on to explain the whole first half of the dance. Cianna listened carefully. "Start the music again, Katie," Polly said.

The music started. The princesses and Cianna danced. They practiced for two hours. Cianna bumped into the girls many times, and she forgot some of the moves. She stepped on Lexi's foot and hit Cidnee in the stomach.

Polly crushed Cianna's toes and said she was sorry. Lexi crashed into her hard enough to knock her off the stage, and Cianna twisted her ankle when she landed.

By the time the two hours were over, Cianna was holding back tears. The dance was hard, Lexi was mean, Cianna felt clumsy, and this was just the first half!

When the music stopped, the princesses collapsed, out of breath. Cianna rested on the window seat where Leroy was now sleeping. She stroked his fluffy fur, listened to horses galloping in a pasture far away, and to Polly's dogs playing together in their kennel. *They might be locked up, but at least they are having fun*, she thought.

No one was chattering now. Polly spoke. "We need a lot more practice before the Spring Festival," she said. "Let's meet every day after lunch for four hours."

The princesses groaned, "Four hours!"

"Four hours," repeated Polly. "I'll see you all tomorrow."

Cianna heard the princesses exit the room one by one. Everyone except Lexi said goodbye to her. Cianna complimented Katie on how well she played the harp.

When Princess Daisy left, she hugged Cianna. "You're a good dancer, don't give up. It takes time to learn *The Seven Sisters*."

Soon Polly and Cianna were alone. "Daisy is right, you did great," Polly reassured her.

Cianna shook her head. "No, I didn't."

Polly sat next to her. "It's a hard dance, Cianna, but you're learning fast. It took Lexi weeks to learn as much as you did today."

"It did?" Cianna was already feeling better.

"Yes, don't worry."

Cianna relaxed. Polly was bossy, but she was also sweet. Daisy and Katie already felt like friends. Everything was going to be okay.

"Since we're going to practice every day, do you want to live at my castle for a while?" Polly asked. "Now that you don't work, you don't have to go back to Flores."

Wow, thought Cianna, *that's a long sleepover!* But Polly was right. She didn't have to go back to Flores for a while. It would be fun to live in the castle. She enjoyed all the pretty smells, she liked Leroy, and she really liked the king and queen. She would miss her little apartment though.

Polly seemed to read her mind. "It's just for two weeks, Cianna."

Cianna didn't have to ask anyone, she took care of herself. She cooked her own food, made her own bed, cleaned her own house, and paid her own bills. But here, at Polly's, the castle staff would take care of her. Cianna made up her mind. "I'd love to stay!"

"Great!"

"But I'll need to go home to pack some clothes and things."

Polly clapped her hands. This was her chance to dress Cianna. "No, I have clothes for you—hair ribbons, shoes, and nightgowns too! I'll give you everything you need."

How kind, thought Cianna, but she needed other things besides clothes, like her favorite blanket, her homemade lotion, and her toothbrush. Also, she'd left her window open and would like to close it. "Thank you, Polly, but I do need a few other things."

"Okay, but no clothes—I will lend you those." Polly didn't want to hurt Cianna's feelings by telling her that her outfits didn't match.

The girls shook hands. "I'll have Caden take you to your apartment tomorrow. It's too late tonight." Polly grabbed Leroy's basket. "Time to go outside, Leroy."

Cianna heard Polly put the dog in his basket and lower him to the grass below. Cianna laughed to herself. She had never known an animal to be so lazy!

When Polly was done, the girls went downstairs for dinner. The king and queen were overjoyed to host Cianna for two weeks, and the king had finally caught a boar. They had salted ham and blueberry pie for dinner.

The sound of the family talking was like music to Cianna, even prettier than Katie's harp.

Nine

~Cianna Rides a Horse~

CIANNA SLEPT in the next day. Getting suspended from work and learning the dance had exhausted her. She woke up alone in Polly's bed, but she knew the castle just well enough to feel her way downstairs. She found Polly and Adeline on the patio. They had saved a plate of pancakes for her.

"Good morning," they greeted Cianna.

"Good morning." Cianna yawned, still tired.

"Did you sleep well?" asked Queen Adeline.

"Yes, Your Highness."

"Please call me Addy. I was going to have Jamie take you into town this morning. He's shopping for a new suit of armor and he's meeting our ship. But he couldn't wait, and I didn't want to wake you. Caden will take you to your apartment today."

"Thank you," said Cianna. "Where's the ship coming from?" Ever since her father disappeared, Cianna liked to keep track of the ships that came and went. She still hoped to hear news of him someday. She would never believe he was gone *forever*.

"It came directly from our kingdom," Polly said, "from Amerok."

Cianna heard the pride in Polly's voice.

"The best swords in the world are made in Amerok," Polly continued. "It's also where books are created. We have lots and lots of trees in my kingdom, and our castle there is ten times bigger than this one."

"It sounds nice," Cianna said. She couldn't imagine why they needed more space when most of the rooms in this castle went unused.

"The ship coming today is bringing more books to sell at the bookshop."

"I wish I could read a book," said Cianna.

"You can't read!"

"Manners, Polly," Adeline snapped.

"There's so much you can't do, Cianna, I don't know how you stand it."

"That's enough," Adeline interrupted. "Please forgive her, Cianna, she speaks without thinking."

"It's okay," Cianna said. "I've never been able to see. And I can read, a little bit."

"How is that?" asked the queen.

"I scratch symbols in my glass bottles at work. I have a different symbol for each of my products. I read the scratches with my fingers and that's how I know which is which."

Adeline was impressed. "You are clever."

Cianna blushed. "Not really."

"Yes, you are. You made up your own way to read. It's wonderful. Well I hope you two have a lovely day, please excuse me." The queen left the table.

Cianna finished her breakfast. "I'm ready to go," she said. "Can I visit the stable while Caden gets the carriage ready?"

"Sure," said Polly. She walked Cianna down the hill and left her by the stable door. "Caden will take care of you now." Polly put Cianna's hand against the doorway.

"Caden!" Polly yelled, "Cianna's here." With that, Polly returned to her castle.

Cianna took in all the different scents. She smelled and heard horses, chickens, and a dog—not Hunter or Leroy—but a strange dog that was in dire need of a bath. She heard more dogs whining in the kennel behind the stable. Footsteps approached her.

"Morning, Cianna," a deep voice greeted her. It was Caden.

"Good morning." She'd been so comfortable with Caden yesterday, but today she felt shy. One of the kennel dogs howled.

"Caden, what does Polly do with all of her dogs?"

Caden laughed at the question, but there was bitterness in his answer. "Nothing," he said. "She just enjoys owning them. Leroy is her favorite, but there are a lot of good dogs in that kennel. I exercise them every day, but they want more than what I can give them."

"What do they want?" Her father was always busy working and taking care of her, so Cianna had never owned a pet.

"They want families to love them."

"Oh," Cianna breathed. She knew how that felt.

Caden changed the subject. "So we're going to your apartment today?" His tension over the dogs eased out of his voice.

"Yes."

"Would you prefer to take the carriage or to ride?"

Cianna frowned. "You mean ... on a horse? Like ride double?"

Caden chuckled. "Yes, but not double. I'll saddle a horse for you."

Cianna gasped and shook her head in surprise that he would even suggest her riding a horse. "I can't ride! And even if I could, how would we carry my things?"

"I'll tie your bag to my saddle. You can ride, Cianna. I'll teach you."

Her father hadn't let her ride alone. It was one of the few things that her blindness had stopped her from doing, but her heart's dream was to ride a horse. Maybe Caden didn't realize she was blind. She'd fooled people before.

"Caden, I can't see anything, nothing at all." A tear rolled down her cheek. "I'm completely blind. Let's just take the carriage." Her shoulders drooped in defeat.

Caden held her hand. "It's okay," he said, using the same tone he used to soothe the horses. "I have a good horse for you. He's kind and gentle, and he can see perfectly well."

Cianna giggled. "Are you serious?" A thrill formed in her belly.

"Yes." Caden squeezed her hand. "I'll get him ready for you. His name is Gildon. Come, you can pet him while I get his saddle."

Caden led Cianna to the horse. He placed her hand on Gildon's shoulder. "You're standing by his front left leg." He walked away to get the saddle.

Cianna slid her hand up his neck and felt her way to his head. He was tall, and his round cheek was the size of a dinner plate! His ears were small and perked. His forehead was wide between his eyes. She let him smell her hand; his breath was hot.

"Ahhhh!" she laughed, delighted. He was licking her fingers! "What does he look like?"

Caden returned and patted Gildon affectionately. "He's brown."

Cianna shook her head. "Can you give me more than that?"

Caden thought a moment. "Okay, he's big."

"I can feel that. Can you tell me anything else?" Obviously, Caden wasn't used to describing horses to blind girls.

Caden closed his eyes. How could he make her see Gildon? "He's smart," Caden said, his eyes still closed, "he respects his rider, he takes careful steps, he's warm, and, uh, he likes to be clean."

Cianna grinned. "He's perfect!"

"I'm riding Spade; he's young and fierce," Caden said, his tone playful. "He's already saddled. Are you ready to go?"

Her father's warnings about riding on her own echoed through her mind. He'd said it wasn't safe. "Are you sure about this?"

"It's going to be fun," Caden promised.

Before Cianna knew what was happening, the stable boy swept her up and placed her gently on the saddle. He arranged her feet in the stirrups and handed her the reins. "I made this saddle for my niece," he said. "It has a high back, leg blocks, and a horn for you to hold on to. It's very secure."

Cianna did feel safe in the saddle, but she resolved to keep a firm grip on the saddle horn.

Caden taught her how to steer one-handed and how to stop the horse. "I'll ride in front of you," he said. "Gildon will follow Spade. Listen for his hoofbeats and relax. You can trust Gildon, he knows what to do."

Cianna loved the feeling of being on the horse. She didn't have to see the ground below to sense how high she was above it.

"Let's go," Caden encouraged her.

His horse walked out of the stable. She'd always loved the sound of hoofbeats on bricks. She squeezed Gildon's sides the way Caden had instructed her. Gildon walked out of the stable and up the hill, following Spade, just as Caden had promised he would. Cianna couldn't believe that she was riding a horse by herself!

They walked in silence for a while. Cianna enjoyed the rocking motion of Gildon's gait. She smelled the flowers and listened to the birds chattering in the trees. Bugs buzzed noisily below, and a flock of geese honked overhead as they returned to Windym for the summer. She felt the gentle heat of the morning sun on her face. It was a beautiful day in her mind, and she was filled with joy.

Cianna was ready for more. "Can we go faster?"

"Already?" Caden asked, surprised. "Sure we can. When you hear me trot Spade, give Gildon a light squeeze. Keep your heels down."

Cianna heard Spade increase his pace. She squeezed Gildon again and he trotted. Cianna bounced wildly in the saddle. She gritted her teeth. *This can't be right*, she thought. She squeezed Gildon again and he cantered; this smoothed out the ride. *Much better!*

"You're cantering!" Caden couldn't believe it. "You were born to ride, Cianna."

She grinned and let the wind wash over her face. She felt Gildon's large muscles contracting under her legs. He was steady. He carried her like a gentleman over the hills, across a bridge, and down the country lanes. Spade and Caden cantered in front of her. She held the reins loosely and let Gildon pick his path. She kept her iron grip on the saddle horn just in case!

Cianna let go of all the worries she carried with her as a blind girl. Every moment of her life she was careful not to trip or bump into things. Now, she relaxed and let this big horse be her legs, and her eyes.

When the pair entered Flores, they slowed the horses to a walk. "Ride next to me," Caden said. She guided Gildon next to him using her ears to see. "I'm proud of you," he said. "Lots of people are afraid of horses."

"I could ride every day of my life," Cianna said. They rode to her apartment, and jaws dropped when the townsfolk saw Cianna riding a horse by herself. Two days ago the blind girl left town with a princess, and today she was riding a huge horse down Port Street. What was next?

Cianna and Caden turned onto Laurel Lane, where Cianna lived above the perfume shop. There was a hitching post there for Caden to tie the horses. He waited while she went upstairs.

Cianna loved her little apartment, but it felt quiet and lonely after her time at the busy castle. She shut the window, packed her bag with lotions and her favorite blanket, locked her door, and returned downstairs. Caden tied the bag to the back of his saddle. "Let's get some ice cream." He grabbed Cianna's hand and pulled her down Laurel Lane.

They crossed Port Street and entered the Snow Globe, where Caden bought each of them a cone. He ordered vanilla with sprinkles for himself. Cianna ordered chocolate with marshmallows on top. They chatted and ate their ice creams outside.

Cianna's shyness from earlier in the morning was gone. Still high from the ride, she entertained Caden with story after story about her job at the Pet Palace. He was amazed by all the different beauty treatments they offered for pets.

"Rabbits get pedicures?" he said, looking down at his own dirty nails.

Cianna understood how silly it sounded.

They finished their ice creams. "We'd better get back," Caden said.

They returned to the horses, and Caden showed Cianna how to mount Gildon by herself. She practiced a few times, and soon she was able to get on and off without assistance. Cianna and Caden rode back to the castle, chatting and laughing the whole way.

When they returned, Polly was outside waiting. "What took you so long?"

"I'm sorry, Princess," Caden said. "I didn't realize it was so late."

"I told you to take the carriage, Caden." Polly huffed. "Cianna can't ride a horse."

"I wanted to ride, Polly, and I can ride a horse. Look at me!" Sometimes it amazed her that she was the blind one.

"I see that you *can* ride, Cianna, but you could have been hurt. I was just worried about you." Polly was younger than Cianna and sometimes it showed.

Cianna slid off Gildon's back. "Please don't worry about me, Polly."

Caden jumped off of Spade and took Cianna's reins. "I had fun," he whispered to her.

"Me too," Cianna whispered back.

Polly wrapped her arm in Cianna's. Her friend was back and she hadn't broken a leg—that was all that mattered. "I laid out a whole new wardrobe for you on my bed. The princesses are already here. I'll help you change, and then it's time to practice."

With that, the two girls went inside the castle.

Ten

~Cianna Runs Away~

THE NEXT TWO WEEKS were busy for Cianna. Every day after lunch she practiced *The Seven Sisters* with the princesses. Polly was right—Cianna learned fast. Soon she was one of the best dancers. Polly moved Cianna to the front of the stage and moved Lexi to the back. Cianna was proud of her dancing, but she wished Polly hadn't given her Lexi's spot.

Polly liked to sleep in every day. Cianna woke early and spent her mornings riding horses with Caden. She also spent time playing with the dogs in Polly's kennel. Soon she knew each one by name, and it wasn't long before she was bathing them, brushing their teeth, and treating their fleas. Cianna sent Caden to the Pet Palace to pick up some of her supplies so she could better care for the neglected dogs. Cianna was always sad when it was time to practice the dance. She disliked leaving the dogs locked in their kennels.

Cianna didn't stop with the dogs. She bathed all the animals in the barn. While Caden did his chores, Cianna bathed the pigs, the horses, the donkey, and the goats. She treated all the barn cats for fleas and worms, made special grains for the older horses, and mixed a pig slop that smelled good even to Caden. Before long the whole stable was filled with clean and happy animals, and the pleasant odor of Cianna's soaps overcame the softer scents of hay and straw.

Cianna's favorite part of the morning was her daily ride with Caden. She and Gildon had learned to trust each other completely. She knew just where to scratch him, and she always had a carrot for him. He let her ride him bareback, and he slept with his head in her lap.

Caden rode a different horse every day, except for Tiara. Polly wouldn't let anyone ride her favorite mare. "It's why she's so wild," Caden explained. "If she let me train her, she would be a better horse."

Cianna believed him. Caden was wonderful with horses. She was there the first time he rode Dash. Dash was Tiara's colt, and he was three years old. Caden worked with him every day from the ground, but the horse had never been ridden. Caden had a special love for Dash; Cianna could hear it in his voice.

One day Caden slid onto Dash's back and that was that. He rode him around the corral without as much as a buck from the young horse.

Caden took Cianna all over Windym during their rides, trotting through the forests, galloping across the meadows, climbing the foothills, and swimming in the cool lakes. Caden described what he saw to Cianna, and she described what she heard and smelled to him. They both learned things they never knew before. Cianna developed into a confident rider, sometimes even taking the lead.

After spending her mornings with Caden and the animals, Cianna lunched with the royal family and then spent her afternoons practicing with the princesses. Cianna enjoyed all the girl talk, even though Lexi ignored her. The princesses taught Cianna about fashion and styling her hair, and her evenings were spent with Polly and her parents. After dinner each night, they sat by the fire, played board games, and drank hot chocolate.

Adeline and Jamie treated Cianna like their own daughter, and Cianna was content. Getting suspended was terrible, but at least she had Caden, the princesses, Adeline, Jamie, and Gildon to make her feel better.

Now it was the day before the Spring Dance. Cianna and Caden had gone on a long ride with the horses that morning. Cianna was tired, but she was also excited. Today was their last dance practice, and it would be a dress rehearsal.

At lunch Cianna asked Polly a question that had been on her mind. "What am I going to wear to the Spring Dance?"

Polly thought for a moment. "Well, I've been wondering the same thing," she said. "We are about the same size, so you will wear one of my dresses, of course. I just haven't decided which one." Polly frowned. All of her dresses were famous, and she wanted Cianna to wear something no one had seen before. "I need to check my closet again."

"Okay," said Cianna. "What are you going to wear?"

Polly clapped her hands with excitement. "I went to town yesterday for my final fitting. My dress is incredible! Mrs. Dunkins is going to sew a few more crystals on it for extra shine. I can't wait! Also, I checked with Jolee about getting Gildon painted for our big entrance tomorrow night, but she said to tell you she's sorry. She couldn't fit him in—not even for me."

"That's okay," Cianna said, relieved. She didn't want Gildon painted or doused in glitter. As much as the royals liked that kind of thing, she knew it just irritated the animals.

Polly snorted. "Not really, Cianna. Of all the horses, Gildon could use some bling. He's quite plain, you know. I guess we could braid some ribbons in his hair."

"Sounds great," Cianna said, but she couldn't care less. She changed the subject before Polly decided to paint Gildon herself. "I bet your dress is very soft." Cianna had been wearing Polly's clothes for two weeks now, and she was amazed at how silky and smooth everything was.

Polly was quiet a moment, remembering the roughness of the mystery cloth. "Well, it's not super-soft," she admitted. "But it is the prettiest dress in the world. It has a rainbow in it—a real rainbow!"

Cianna had heard about rainbows. She knew they were special and wonderful. Her father told her once that if he had a wish, he would ask for Cianna to be able to see things like rainbows and sunsets—things that couldn't be smelled or touched. He said the heavens had never created anything more beautiful or elusive than the rainbow.

Cianna would like to see one too, but she wouldn't waste a wish on it. She would ask for her father back. "I'm sure your dress will be the prettiest in the seven kingdoms," she said.

"Of course it will."

Just then the castle bell rang. Cianna heard that sound a lot in this house. Adeline and Polly had something delivered to them almost every day.

"It's my dress!" Polly ran to answer the door.

Cianna chased after her as best she could. She knew the castle pretty well now.

Polly threw open the huge front door and spoke to a delivery man. She signed her name on a slip of paper. He left, and Polly had her dress. "Let's go upstairs," she said. "I want to try it on again."

The two girls skipped up the stairs. Cianna was excited even though she couldn't see the gown. They entered Polly's room and the princess slammed the door. She ripped open her package.

"Oh," Polly said. "It's beautiful." She put on the dress and twirled in front of her mirror. She couldn't believe her eyes. She was wearing a rainbow! The sparkling white dress lit up Polly's room. The rainbow struggled to escape, but it was sewn tight to the fabric. The crystals sparkled like dewdrops, and the blue lace was the color of the sky. This year she would blow everyone away. "You can touch it," Polly said.

Cianna walked over and touched the dress. She hid her gasp. The skirt of the gown was full and it hung on Polly like a big bell, but it was so scratchy! It felt like sandpaper. "I wish I could see it," Cianna said. *It must look better than it feels*, she thought.

Polly took the dress off. "I'm going to hide it," she said. "I don't want anyone to see it until the dance. Of course, you don't count, because you didn't actually see it."

Cianna ignored the comment. Sometimes Polly hurt her feelings when she spoke without thinking.

Polly wrapped her dress in paper and hid it in the back of her closet. While she was in there, she found her old cloud dress. It was the only gown she had never worn to an event; it would be perfect for Cianna. She came out of the closet with the dress. "Look what I found."

"What is it?" *Why did people always ask her to look at things!*

"It's my cloud dress. You can wear it to the dance. Try it on." Polly handed Cianna the dress.

As soon as Cianna touched the cloud fabric, she loved it. It was softer than rabbit fur, and it was light and cool. She put it on and twirled, feeling the dress billow around her like air.

"It fits you well enough." Polly tried to describe the dress. "It's kind of a light gray with lots of silver lining. It's plain, but that's okay. It shows off your beautiful hair. I'll get you some shoes." Polly retrieved a pair of silver spidersilk slippers from her closet. They also fit Cianna.

"Now you just need jewelry." Polly rustled through her jewelry case. "These will do." Polly chose a matching set of fresh water pearls connected by silver beads and small crystals. She put the earrings, necklace, and bracelet on Cianna. "Just one more thing," she said. She fixed Cianna's hair with a pearl clip. Polly stepped back and took in the full effect. "Wow, you look great." Polly wasn't kidding. "You look like a princess."

Cianna felt like a princess. She had never worn jewelry before, or slippers, or a cloud dress. "I love all of it, Polly."

The girls heard the castle bell ring. "The princesses are here!" Polly squealed.

Sure enough, the princesses had arrived. Cianna heard them gallop up the stairs. Polly opened her door and the princesses rushed in, chattering like birds in the morning. When they saw Cianna, a hush came over the room.

Cianna sensed the girls staring at her, and her cheeks flamed. Katie was the first to speak. "Is that Cianna?"

"It sure is." Polly was proud of her beautiful town girl.

"You look lovely," Katie marveled. The princesses murmured their agreement, except Lexi.

"Cloud dresses are out this year," she sneered. "And it's supposed to have a rainbow in it. A cloud dress is boring without a rainbow."

The other princesses were silent.

Lexi snorted. "I guess it doesn't make any difference to you, Cianna, since you can't see."

Katie and Daisy gasped.

Cianna's cheeks burned hotter. Polly hurt her feelings, but never on purpose. Lexi was just plain mean. Cianna couldn't think of anything to say. She felt a lump in her throat. *Don't cry*, she told herself.

Polly clapped her hands. "Let's change into our costumes and start practice," she said.

Polly handed Cianna a costume, and they all changed. Cianna couldn't see her outfit. She pulled on leggings, a short skirt, and a sleeveless fitted top. She was too upset to care how she looked in it.

The girls climbed onto Polly's stage. Cianna heard the swish of short skirts. She didn't feel like dancing, but she knew the princesses needed her, and she didn't want to let them down. Besides, she wasn't a quitter. Katie started the music.

The girls practiced for hours. Lexi bumped into Cianna over and over again. Cianna tired to ignore it. Finally, Lexi shoved Cianna so hard she flew off the stage and landed on the carpet. Cianna had not fallen off the stage since the very first practice. Polly saw what happened.

"Lexi," she scolded, "say sorry to Cianna. You did that on purpose."

Cianna lay on the floor with a hurt elbow. She hid her sadness. "I'm okay." She wasn't going to let Lexi get to her.

"You see, she's okay," said Lexi.

"You should still say sorry."

Lexi stomped her foot. "Well, I won't say sorry to her, Polly. She's not one of us. She's a town girl, and if she can't handle it, she should leave!" Lexi was breathing hard, almost crying. "And she's blind! You guys think she looks pretty, well I think she looks creepy!" Lexi ran into Polly's bathroom and slammed the door.

Cianna's heart pounded. Katie dropped her harp with a sharp twang. Cianna's eyes filled with tears, and she couldn't breathe. Everyone was stunned, and no one stood up for her. Cianna would not let them see her cry. She stepped gracefully off the stage and walked out of Polly's room.

In the hallway, Cianna's tears came in a flood. It was nighttime now, and she had nowhere to go. She heard someone singing. It was Adeline.

Cianna rushed toward the queen's voice. Using her hands, she felt her way through a large bedroom and into a bathroom. She guessed it was a bathroom because she heard water running. "Addy, are you here?" she asked.

"Yes, Cianna, I'm right here."

The queen was sitting by the tub in her robe and Cianna collapsed in her arms. Adeline hugged her while she sobbed. "What happened?" the queen asked.

Cianna shook her head. She didn't want to talk about it. Adeline stroked her hair, soothing her. After a while, Cianna stopped crying.

"Your costume is adorable," Adeline said.

"Thank you." Cianna sniffled.

The two talked for a while in the bathroom about everything except what had just happened in Polly's room. They discussed Cianna's job, riding horses, and even her missing father. Adeline held Cianna's hands until she relaxed and began to feel better.

They heard the castle bell ring. "Who could that be?" wondered Adeline.

The family butler answered the door. He trotted up the stairs and informed Adeline that a message had arrived for Polly. "She's in her room," said Adeline.

Adeline pulled Cianna up. "I know one thing that's true, Cianna: Polly adores you. You are like a big sister to her. I don't know what happened in there, but just know that Polly is your friend."

Cianna took a deep breath. "Okay," she said. Then Cianna froze; she smelled something familiar. It took Cianna just a second to place the odor. It was the tar smell! It was the same scent she'd detected in her shampoo bottle when Peaches's hair came off. Now it lingered on the queen. "What's that smell?" asked Cianna.

Adeline looked around her and grabbed an open bottle. "You mean this?" She handed the bottle to Cianna.

Cianna smelled it. "Yes, what is that?" Her heart was beating wildly.

"It's a new cream for getting rid of hair," the queen said. "I don't have to shave my legs anymore! Princess Anna gave it to me."

Cianna gasped. "Hair-removing cream, from Princess Anna?" Her world grew clearer and crashed down on her at the same time.

"Yes, and it works great. Why?"

"Never mind," Cianna grunted. "I'm ready to practice the dance again. Thank you, Addy."

Adeline hugged her again. "Sweet dreams tonight," she said.

Cianna walked out of Adeline's room with her hands balled into fists. Princess Anna had put the hair-removing cream in her shampoo. Princess Anna had made sure her own rat's hair fall out. Princess Anna had gotten Cianna suspended *on purpose*. It had all been planned so that Cianna would be free to take Mirabel's place in the dance. Cianna was furious.

The princesses had used her. They didn't care about her at all. Cianna stormed down the hallway. She would give them a piece of her mind! When she got to Polly's room, she heard the girls talking. Cianna listened at the door.

Polly was ripping open the envelope from the butler. "It's a note from Mirabel," she said.

"Read it!" Lexi urged. She must have come out of the bathroom.

Polly read the note out loud:

Dearest Polly,
It's a miracle! I'm healed.
I no longer have the pox.
I will attend the Spring Festival
and I have been practicing the dance.
May I still perform with all

of you tomorrow?
Your friend, Mirabel

"That's great news!" Lexi cheered, and the princesses agreed. They were all happy Mirabel was feeling better.

"Everything has worked out perfectly," said Princess Anna.

"But what about Cianna?" asked Princess Daisy.

"We don't need her anymore," Lexi said. "It wouldn't look good to dance with a town girl anyway. Polly can send her back to Flores in the morning."

"Don't you think that will make Cianna sad?" Katie pointed out.

"Yes, she'll be sad," said Daisy. "She's worked so hard."

"She'll get over it," answered Lexi "Will you send her away, Polly?"

Polly thought about it. "I don't know what to do. I like Cianna a lot, but I can't say no to Mirabel either. She's my oldest friend." Polly sighed. "Lexi is right about one thing: Cianna is not a princess like us. After the Spring Festival, she's going back to work and we're going home to our kingdoms. We won't see her for another year."

"Cianna knows that," said Lexi. "She's lucky she got to hang out with us at all."

Polly made up her mind. "Fine, I'll tell Cianna in the morning. I'll give her some more of my clothes, I'm sure that will make her feel better."

Cianna slumped against the hallway wall and cried silently into her hands. She didn't know what hurt more—that she would miss the Spring Dance or that her new friends had used her.

Then Polly's door opened. Cianna ducked behind a pillar. She heard the princesses say goodbye and leave the room. They went down the stairs and out the front door where their carriages waited to take them home. Cianna stayed hidden.

"I wonder where Cianna went," Polly said to herself.

Polly's footsteps pattered down the hallway. When she was out of earshot, Cianna slipped back into her bedroom. She couldn't breathe. She had been furious, and now she was heartbroken. She had to get away. She ran to the open window. How could she get down? Her hand touched Leroy's basket. *That's it*, she thought. Cianna would escape using Leroy's basket.

She heard Polly returning, calling her name. "Cianna! Where are you?"

There was no time! Cianna stripped off the costume, which would be for Mirabel now, and grabbed the first garment she could find— it was the cloud dress. Cianna pulled it on. She was still wearing the jewels, the pearl hair clip, and the slippers. Oh well, she would return them later; right now she had to get away!

Cianna hopped into the basket and lowered herself to the ground. She climbed out on the lawn and listened. No one was outside. She heard a horse whinny. *Maybe Gildon will take me home?*

Cianna walked carefully down the hill. Regular people could not see well in the dark, but it made no difference to her. Caden had told her horses could see well in the dark, and she hoped he was right.

Cianna slipped into the stable and went to Gildon's stall. He licked her fingers. "Will you take me home?" He nickered. Cianna opened his stall door, careful to be quiet. Caden was asleep upstairs, and she didn't want to wake him.

Cianna stood on an overturned bucket, grabbed Gildon's mane, and pulled herself onto his bare back. It was hard to do wearing the cloud dress. Once she was seated, she squeezed his sides. "Take me home," she whispered to him.

Gildon trotted out of the stable and away from the castle. The night was lonely and cold. Gildon felt like her only friend in the world. Cianna hugged his neck and soaked up his warmth. The gentle horse carried her home.

Eleven

~Dressing for the Dance~

CIANNA ARRIVED at the town gates in the middle of the night. She slid off Gildon. "Thank you." She kissed his nose. Her tears had dried, but she felt empty. She hugged Gildon's neck. "I'm back where I belong," she said. "Now you need to go back to where you belong. I left your stall door open." She turned him around and gave him a pat on his rear. Gildon seemed to know what she wanted, and he trotted back toward Polly's castle.

The main gates of Flores were huge and made of iron. Large carriages could fit between them during the day, but now they were locked. Cianna knew of a smaller gate made of wood for people on foot, and it was never locked. She entered Flores and took in the familiar salty smell of the village.

The streets were mostly quiet. Cianna heard some people talking through open windows. Sad notes from a piano drifted from above, and a few grownups were telling stories on a front porch. Cianna walked carefully home. She kept the key to her apartment on a piece of twine around her ankle. She used it now to unlock her door.

She couldn't help but smile when she walked inside. *I'm home*, she thought. It was a little stuffy, but it smelled just like she remembered. Cianna opened her large window and let the warm night air brush her cheek.

Tomorrow evening she would hear all the lovely sounds of the Spring Dance from this window, just like every year in the past. She'd thought all her dreams were coming true— she'd met a new friend, been part of a family, and enjoyed dinners with a mother and a father, even if they weren't her own. She'd learned how to ride a horse, and she was going to attend the Spring Dance. Now it was all ruined. Cianna didn't have any tears left to cry. She curled into a ball on her window seat. Before long, she was asleep.

~ ~ ~ ~ ~

Early the next morning, Caden ran as fast as he could up the hill to Polly's castle. He rang the bell, and Queen Adeline answered the door. Caden's eyes were wide, and he was breathing hard.

Queen Adeline frowned. "Caden, what happened?" she asked.

"I don't know," he said. "I found Gildon loose in the barn, and his stall door is open. I know I locked him in last night. I can't imagine how he got out, unless someone took him for a ride."

Caden and Adeline both knew who that someone might be, but Cianna was with Polly. "You must have forgotten to shut the door, Caden," Adeline reasoned. "Cianna is here."

"Please check," begged Caden.

Queen Adeline yelled for Polly. Polly ran downstairs in her blue flowercloth nightgown. She looked guilty. Queen Adeline crossed her arms. "Where is Cianna, Polly? Is she with you?"

Polly didn't say anything. She just shrugged.

"Polly, answer me," Adeline snapped. "Where is she?"

"I'm not exactly sure," answered Polly. "I think she got mad and ran away."

Adeline sucked in her breath. Caden's heart sped up a notch. Adeline gripped her daughter's arms. "Why didn't you come and tell me, Polly? This is serious. Cianna could be hurt somewhere."

Polly stared at the ground and said nothing.

"Did you know that she came into my room crying last night?"

Polly shook her head.

"What were you two fighting about?"

Polly didn't know if Cianna had heard the discussion about Mirabel or not, but she hadn't meant to hurt her feelings on purpose so Polly decided not to mention it. Instead, she blamed Lexi. "Lexi pushed her down and said she looked creepy."

Caden sucked in his breath, and Adeline rolled her eyes. "Well, it's done. Now we need to find her. Polly, you're grounded until this evening. Go to your room and stay there. If your dance wasn't part of tonight's program, I wouldn't let you go at all."

Adeline was fond of Cianna. She'd always wanted more children after Polly, but it didn't happen. She liked having another child in the castle, and she was furious with Polly for not telling anyone that their guest had run away. Cianna was blind and she could be in great danger.

Polly turned and stomped up the stairs. "It's not fair!" she yelled. "The jousting finals are this morning, and I'm missing everything!" She slammed her huge solid-wood door.

Adeline turned to Caden. "You take Spade and search the forests. Jamie will search the hills with Hunter. I'll take Mina and check Cianna's apartment."

"Yes, Your Highness." Caden nodded. He imagined Cianna lying in the forest somewhere, hurt and alone, unable to see. Fear for her gripped him. He ran back to the stable to ready the horses.

Soon Caden, Adeline, and Jamie galloped away in three different directions. All that mattered was finding Cianna.

~ ~ ~ ~ ~

Cianna woke to a knock on her door. She sat up, and rubbed her eyes. "Who is it?"

"It's Addy," said the queen with relief.

Cianna opened the door, allowing Adeline to enter. The queen grabbed Cianna and hugged her. "I'm so glad you aren't hurt," she said. "We've been looking all over for you."

Cianna felt terrible. She hadn't meant for anyone to worry. "I'm sorry."

"Don't be sorry!" Adeline exclaimed. "How are you? Do you want to talk about it?"

Cianna let the queen hold her. It felt so nice to be hugged, but Cianna didn't want to tell Adeline what Polly and her friends had done. It was too much.

It didn't matter now anyway. The dance was tonight, and she would have her job back tomorrow. Everything would go back to the way it was. Cianna had been silly to think her dreams were coming true. Wonderful things didn't happen to her, only sad things. "I really don't want to talk about it," Cianna insisted gently.

Adeline wiped Cianna's hair out of her eyes. "All right, you don't have to tell me, dear." Adeline looked at Cianna with renewed admiration. Cianna had the saddest face and the biggest green eyes—it was agony for Adeline to see her hurt. The queen realized she was more attached to Cianna than she'd ever imagined. "Are you still coming to the Spring Dance tonight?"

Cianna shook her head. "No. Mirabel is healthy, they don't need me anymore."

The queen began to understand how Cianna must be feeling—like the princesses had used her and then abandoned her. Adeline pursed her lips. She was going to have a long talk with her daughter.

Cianna motioned toward her bed. "Will you please take this cloud dress and these jewels back to Polly?" The dress, the jewels, the pearl clip, and the slippers were arranged neatly on top of her blankets.

"No," insisted Addy. "Keep the dress. I bought it, not Polly. It's mine, and I'm giving it to you. Keep the slippers and the jewelry also."

"I can't!"

"Yes, you can!" the queen said. "That's an order. Take these also." Adeline pressed two articles of scented paper in her hands.

"What are these?" Cianna asked.

"Two tickets to the Spring Dance," Adeline explained, patting Cianna. "Please come and bring a friend."

Cianna was speechless.

"I insist that you come," said Adeline. "You will be my guest, not Polly's. Okay?"

Cianna didn't want to be around Polly and her friends. "Can I think about it?" she asked.

"Of course," said the queen. "Now that I know you're okay, I have to go. I need to let Jamie and Caden know you're safe, and I have to pick up Leroy and Tiara from the Pet Palace. Polly had them painted some crazy colors. Poor things!" Adeline kissed Cianna and left the apartment.

Cianna fixed herself breakfast. She would talk to Mia later about the tickets.

~ ~ ~ ~ ~

That evening every royal in Windym was dressing for the dance. Princes and princesses everywhere were buttoning dresses, polishing swords, buckling boots, and clipping on earrings.

In Flores, the townsfolk prepared for a party of their own. This year, the Flores Town Council voted to close Port Street and celebrate the end of spring with a giant block party. There would be music, dancing, yummy food, and games for the kids.

Mia was at Cianna's apartment admiring the scented golden dance tickets. "You have to go!" Mia insisted. "Don't worry about those spoiled princesses. This is your night, Cianna, and this dress is amazing." Mia sank her fingers into the cloud gown again. "You have the dress, the jewelry, the shoes, the tickets—you just have to attend!"

"Will you go with me?"

Mia sighed. "Oh Cianna, I would love to, you know I would, but I promised to help with the block party." Mia patted Cianna's leg. "Besides, I don't have a dress and it's too late to get one. All the shops are closed."

"Who will go with me?"

Mia played with Cianna's hair. "The queen said you will be her guest. She'll take care of you. Please go, Cianna. After what those girls did to you, you deserve this night." Cianna had told Mia everything.

"Do you think Polly knows what Anna did?" Mia asked.

Cianna shrugged. "I don't know, Mia. I hope not."

"So will you go to the dance?"

It *was* Cianna's dream to attend. She *did* have two tickets and a dress. Her father *had* taught her that no person was better than another, no matter how much money they had or how well they could see. She decided that being royal did not make the princesses better than her. She felt her fighting spirit return. "Yes, I will go," she decided.

"That's my girl!" cried Mia. "Now, let's get you cleaned up."

Cianna took a bath while Mia fluffed out the cloud dress. When Cianna was clean and dry, she stepped into the gown. Mia helped her with the jewelry, the slippers, some makeup, and she styled Cianna's hair.

Mia liked to play with hair. She often came over to eat with Cianna and to practice on her long bronze locks. Mia kept a supply of products in Cianna's apartment for those nights. Mia's dream was to open a hair salon someday.

Tonight she streaked Cianna's red hair with silver highlights to match the silver lining in the dress. She created loose curls and styled them up, securing them with the pearl hair clip. She pulled long tendrils down to frame Cianna's face and delicate shoulders. She sprayed her hair with jasmine-scented glitter. Mia stepped back. "You are stunning, Cianna."

Next, Mia painted Cianna's fingernails with rainbow polish. "For some color!" she explained. She painted Cianna's toenails too, and brushed her lips with shimmering gloss. When she was finished, Mia handed Cianna a gift.

Cianna fingered the box in her hand. "What is this?" she asked, surprised.

"I got it to cheer you up after you were suspended. I just hadn't given it to you yet," Mia said. "Open it!"

Cianna opened the box, and inside was a glass bottle. She removed the lid, smelled the liquid inside, and lost her breath. "It's Unicornia perfume!" She'd never owned her own bottle of perfume before, and she lived above a perfume shop! "Thank you, Mia!" Cianna hugged her friend.

"You're welcome," said Mia. She placed a drop of the perfume on each of Cianna's wrists and behind each earlobe. "Now, let's rent you a rickshaw and get you to that dance."

Cianna and Mia went outside and Mia whistled for a rickshaw driver. People walking on the street stopped and stared at Cianna. "They're admiring you," Mia told her.

When Cianna climbed into the rickshaw and pulled away, the townsfolk clapped for her. Cianna could not see them, but she waved anyway. Tears of joy filled her eyes. She was going to the Spring Dance!

~ ~ ~ ~ ~

Meanwhile, Polly was in her bedroom at the castle. She was also dressing for the dance. She put on her new rainbow gown and glass slippers and twirled in front of the mirror. The trapped rainbow rippled across the sparkling fabric. Polly was thrilled until she stopped twirling. The fabric poked at her through the lining, irritating her skin. Polly scratched her leg. Then she scratched her other leg. Wow, she didn't remember the dress being so itchy. She did her best to ignore it.

Polly put on her aquamarine necklace and earrings, which complemented her gloves and the lace trim on her dress. She sprayed her black curls with rainbow glitter, put a small diamond tiara on her head, and smiled at the pretty girl in the mirror. She looked perfect.

"Come on, Leroy, it's time to go."

Leroy's curly coat was brushed out and dyed blue. He resembled a walking cotton ball. His nails were painted white, and he had a white bow on his head. He was not thrilled, he just wanted to go back to sleep.

Polly snapped a white crystal-studded leash to his collar and led him downstairs. Adeline and Jamie were waiting for her. Polly scratched her arms. *So itchy!*

"You look lovely, Polly," said her mother coolly.

Adeline had informed Polly earlier that Cianna was safe at home and that she was going to have a long chat with Polly after the dance. Polly wasn't looking forward to the lecture, but she did feel better knowing Cianna was safe.

Her father kissed her cheek. "Look at that dress!" he said.

The three of them went outside. Caden was there with the family's royal carriage. It was pink and pulled by a pair of twin black horses. The horses each wore a large pink feather, like a hat, between their ears. Caden was dressed in a fancy white suit to drive the carriage. He had also heard the news that Cianna was safe in her apartment. He tried not to glower at Polly when he saw her. She didn't look sorry to him. But Cianna was safe, and that was all that mattered.

Tiara was saddled and waiting, but she was in a sour mood. The thick colorful paint bothered her, and she tossed her head.

Polly gasped when she saw her white mare. Jolee had outdone herself! Every inch of Tiara was colored in striped pastels and brushed with glitter. "Wow!" Polly squealed.

"Maybe you should ride in the carriage," suggested Caden. "Tiara can walk behind it until she cools off." It was still his job to manage the horses. *If only Polly would let me ride that crazy mare*, he thought, *I could train her to behave.*

Polly ignored him, still admiring her horse. As Tiara danced around, the painted rainbows danced with her. The mare matched Polly's dress perfectly, and her mane and tail were braided with sky-blue ribbons. Polly couldn't wait to show up at the dance riding Tiara with Leroy in her lap. Daisy was brilliant to think of it!

"Help me up," Polly ordered Caden, too bedazzled by her mare to notice the flared nostrils.

"Yes, Your Highness." Caden glanced at Jamie and Adeline.

They nodded to him. Against his better judgment, he helped Polly onto her irritated horse. Next went Leroy. The dog whined and struggled as Caden handed him to Polly. She lodged him securely against her stomach, but the little dog looked at Caden with mild terror in his eyes. Polly just laughed.

Caden opened the carriage door for the king and queen. When they were settled, he gave a soft cluck to the carriage horses and they pulled away from the castle at a slow trot. The movement seemed to calm Tiara. She pranced, but she didn't buck or bolt. *Maybe they will be okay*, thought Caden.

As they headed to Sweet Hall, Caden glanced back at the stable. No one else noticed the brown gelding standing in the shadows. It was Gildon, loose again. He held his head high as he sniffed the wind. A small saddle was strapped to his back. This time it was Caden who'd freed the horse. "You know where she is," Caden whispered, "go get her."

~ ~ ~ ~ ~

Cianna was gliding down a country road in the rickshaw when she heard galloping hooves.

"That's odd," said the rickshaw driver. "A big brown horse is coming straight at us." The driver stopped to assess the strange horse. "He's wearing a saddle!"

"Gildon?" Cianna wondered aloud. The horse nickered so she climbed out of the rickshaw.

"Careful, miss, that's a big horse."

"It's okay, I think I know him." Cianna held out her hand. The plain brown horse came to a halt, dropped his nose into her palm, and licked her fingers. Cianna grinned. "It's him! It's Gildon." She caressed his cheek. "You came for me, didn't you, boy?" He nickered again.

Cianna was delighted. "This is my ride to the dance," she told the driver.

"Miss, I don't think it's safe for you to ride that horse. He doesn't even have a bridle."

Cianna giggled. "That's okay, he knows where we're going better than I do."

"But it's getting dark, miss." The sun had just dropped below the horizon.

Cianna laughed. "It's always dark in my world." She grabbed Gildon's mane, slipped her foot into the stirrup, and swung herself, dress and all, onto Gildon's back. Mia had already paid the driver so Cianna excused him. "Thank you, sir, and have a nice evening!"

Cianna grabbed the horn, squeezed Gildon, and they cantered away. The driver shook his head in wonder.

Gildon carried her toward the distant sound of music. She would arrive at the dance on horseback, just like the princesses. The evening was still warm, a few birds were singing, and Cianna's heart swelled with joy. She was riding a horse, dressed in a cloud, and she was on her way to the Spring Dance!

Twelve

~Arriving at Sweet Hall~

POLLY AND HER FAMILY were almost to the Spring Dance. Every year it was held at Sweet Hall, a building on top of the tallest foothill. A long winding path led to the building, and it was lined on each side with pretty lamps. Polly and Tiara rode in front of her parents' carriage. As they approached the top of the hill, Sweet Hall came into view.

It was beautiful in the moonlight. Firefly lamps lit up the building, rose petals carpeted the walkways, and flags from each of the seven kingdoms decorated the turrets. Soft music filtered through the windows, and a large fountain bubbled in the center of the front lawn.

She noticed Prince Jayson in the distance. He was sipping punch on a low balcony, and his black hair was tied back with a royal-blue ribbon. She wondered how he'd fared in the jousting finals that morning. He and his palomino had been favored to win.

Everyone liked to wait outside to watch the royal and wealthy families arrive. Sketch artists drew their impressions of the guests as they exited their carriages, capturing all the fashion hits and misses. The best outfit of the evening would grace the cover of the next issue of *Princess Style* magazine.

The carriages and horses were also worth looking at on this night. Polly's carriage had been painted, polished, and decorated with pink satin ribbons and silver bells. The horses were glistening and their hooves shone with black oil. Everyone and everything looked their best. Polly couldn't wait for the reaction when she arrived wearing a rainbow dress and riding a painted mare.

"Psst!" someone hissed at Polly.

"Who's there?"

"It's me, Lexi. Come over here, we're all waiting for you."

Polly spotted Lexi in the shadows. The plan was for Polly to arrive with her friends. They were hiding and waiting for her in a grove of trees. "Go on without me," Polly said to her parents.

The carriage rolled past. "We'll see you inside," said the king.

Polly rode Tiara into the shadows with Lexi. All her friends were there. Polly looked them over with joy. Daisy wore a yellow gown made entirely of ruffles. Her pet lovebird, George, rode on her shoulder. He wore a yellow smoking jacket. Her horse, Calvin, had yellow highlights in his chestnut hair, and his saddle blanket was as ruffled as her gown.

Princess Cidnee wore an emerald-green spidersilk dress. Thousands of tiny opals encrusted the long skirt. The green dress showed off Cidnee's dark waves of hair, and her olive skin was radiant. Polly had always envied Cidnee and Daisy for their dark skin— they looked great in every color!

Cidnee carried her silver fox, Dandy, on her lap. Dandy wore an opal crown between her ears and an opal bracelet on each leg. Cidnee's black mare, Maddie, had bright green polka dots painted all over her. Polly nodded her approval.

Princess Laci wore a pale orange satin gown. The hem and the capped sleeves were trimmed with white fur and the cut of the dress was slim. Laci's pet meerkat, Mipsy, had wrapped herself around Laci's neck, looking like another fur accessory. The meerkat wore a matching orange satin dress. Laci's white horse was shimmering in orange glitter, and the same glitter decorated Laci's platinum-blond hair. They looked fabulous.

Princess Anna was stunning in a dark sapphire dress. A transparent spidersilk shawl covered her shoulders. Anna's dark blond hair was piled high atop her head. She had pinned brilliant sapphires and diamonds throughout her curls. Anna's rat, Peaches, rode in her purse. Most of Peaches's hair had grown back. He was dressed in a tuxedo with dark blue accents.

Anna's horse also had real diamonds and sapphires pinned in his mane and tail and across his saddle blanket. Anna had gone all out with the jewels this year! Of course, her kingdom of Wilaysia was famous for its abundance of precious gems.

Princess Mirabel looked a bit pale in her dark purple dress. The pox had kept her indoors for weeks, and even her freckles were lighter. Her dark red hair, the same color as Cianna's, hung in loose waves. Tiny purple flowers were woven throughout her locks, and hundreds of real flowers in every color were sewn into the transparent hem of her dress.

Her pet cheetah, Trixi, followed her on the ground. Jolee had painted wildflowers on the cheetah and each of her spots was the center of a flower. Mirabel's horse, Thunder, had purple flowers woven in his black mane and tail, and purple polish colored his hooves.

And then there was her best friend, Lexi. Polly looked her up and down, and Lexi looked Polly up and down. Lexi wore a glimmering pastel gown. It was all the colors at once. Polly had never seen anything like it. She guessed it was the new fabric from Manlaya that everyone was talking about. It looked like the inside of a seashell, but the colors changed as Lexi moved. Polly blinked, not believing her eyes, and Lexi smirked as though she had a secret. As Polly stared, the dress turned dark pink.

Lexi laughed at the look on Polly's face. "Jorge designed it," she boasted.

Polly hadn't heard of Jorge in years. He used to be Manlaya's best designer and inventor. One year he just disappeared. Everyone thought he'd retired.

Lexi preened herself. "He's been working on this fabric since I was two years old. It's a mood dress."

"It's amazing," Polly said. She made a mental note to get a mood dress as soon as possible, and she didn't care how much it cost her mother.

The other princesses were just as stunned. Lexi's dress was dazzling. As the princesses complimented Lexi, the pink dress changed to violet.

Lexi's black bear, Lucy, wore a matching mood collar that was currently misty blue. Lexi's palomino had hundreds of crystal beads woven into her mane and tail and across her saddle pad to reflect whatever color Lexi's dress happened to be, which depended on Lexi's mood. Right now the shiny crystals set off a violet sparkle. Polly was annoyed that Lexi had found this new style first, but she still thought her rainbow dress was better and rarer.

Polly fluffed her own dress and angled herself to catch the full light of the moon.

The princesses turned their attention to her now, and their mouths dropped. They hadn't noticed the shy rainbow in her dress until the moonlight exposed its pale stripes. "Is that a real rainbow?" whispered Laci.

"Yes, it is," Polly bragged.

"I've never seen a rainbow up close," whispered Anna.

"I've never seen a prettier horse up close," said Cidnee, noting the complex rainbow stripes painted on Tiara.

Lexi's dress was all but forgotten. The mood dress was interesting, but the rainbow dress was magical. Each princess touched Polly's dress, hoping for some rainbow luck.

The rainbow swirled around, trying to hide from them, which created the illusion that Polly's skirt was spinning.

"You look better than I do," complained Lexi. Her mood dress turned green.

Polly beamed. "Thanks!"

Just then Laci's sister, Princess Katie, rode up on her little red pony, Comet. She wore a pink-and-white dress loaded with frills and satin ribbons. Comet wore a pink bow on her tail, and Katie had braided matching ribbons through her mane. Katie's harp was strapped to her back, and her gray eyes twinkled. "Can I join you guys?"

Lexi frowned, and her dress lightened to orange. "Not on that pony," she said. "You don't fit in, Katie."

"Okay," said Katie, but she sounded disappointed.

Laci scowled at Lexi and turned to her little sister. "You can do us a favor, Katie. Will you go up to Sweet Hall and let everyone know we're coming?"

Katie brightened. "Sure, I can do that." She clucked to her pony, and they trotted up the firefly path to Sweet Hall. Katie asked an usher to announce the coming arrival of Polly and her friends. There was a hush as all the royals and the wealthy families turned to watch for them.

In their grove of trees, the princesses heard the usher's loud announcement. "Are you ready, girls?" Polly asked.

"We're ready," they said together.

Polly and her friends left the trees and rode side by side on the path leading to Sweet Hall. Polly rode in the center. Anna, Lexi, and Cidnee were on her right side. Laci, Mirabel, and Daisy rode on her left. As soon as they came into view, the crowd gasped.

The princesses were lovely. The crowd was amazed by the fancy dresses, the matching horses, and the pretty pets. The girls stopped and posed. The Spring Dance artists whipped out their sketchpads and quickly drew every detail.

Polly urged Tiara a few steps ahead of the group. The full light of Sweet Hall's huge lanterns washed over them. She grinned at Prince Jayson, who had frozen in mid-sentence to stare at her. The young prince he'd been speaking with froze too. The princesses had outdone themselves this year.

Polly noticed the jousting medal around Prince Jayson's neck, so he had won the tournament! Polly felt irritated all over again for missing the finals that morning. She remembered why she missed it and felt a pain in her stomach when she thought of Cianna, but Polly ignored it. This was her moment!

The crowd whispered about Polly's amazing dress. The rainbow was fully exposed now, to everyone's delight. It trembled in the rough fabric and cast tiny versions of itself all around her. The royals clapped their gloved hands. Tiara pranced in place and snorted. The clapping and all the attention stressed her, and the dry paint on her body made her itch. She tossed her mane.

All eyes were on Polly when a young prince who wasn't paying attention to the pretty girls decided to light the firecracker he had just purchased from the souvenir shack. He stuck the wick in a table candle until the wick caught fire. He watched the little flame get closer and closer to the fire powder. When it was too close for comfort, the little prince threw the firecracker into the air. It landed right next to Tiara's hoof. **CRACK!** The firecracker exploded.

Shock rippled through the mare, and she reared. Polly screamed, clinging to Tiara's neck, "Whoa!"

The other horses pranced, but they didn't run. Princess Anna gasped, and Lexi's dress turned yellow. Caden was tending Polly's carriage horses, so he was too far away to help.

The firecracker threw off one last popping spark, and Tiara bolted. She galloped straight for the fountain, dropped her neck, and skidded to a halt. Polly and Leroy flew off her back, and landed with a splash in the cool water.

Tiara trotted frantically around the fountain and then dropped to her knees on the lawn. She rolled and rolled, trying to rub off the thick paint that made her so itchy. With green grass stains now marring her pretty rainbow painting, Tiara stood up, shook hard, and galloped home to the quiet warmth of her stall.

Meanwhile, Polly struggled in the fountain. The water had soaked and ruined her new dress. Her hair was stuck to her head, flat and wet and her crown had fallen off and rolled under a bush. Leroy was barking and splashing. The dye washed out of his fur and stained the water and Polly's white dress blue. She burst into tears. King Jamie rescued her and Leroy from the fountain, and Polly fell into his arms.

Everyone was whispering about her, and a few younger children laughed. "Mama!" sobbed Polly.

Adeline was near, and she hugged her daughter. *You should have listened to Caden*, she thought.

Leroy shook off the water and trotted away from Polly in search of a nice dry place to take a nap.

The crowd turned their backs on the scene and returned to gossiping. Polly's friends slid off their horses and huddled together with their pets, meek and miserable. Caden returned. He looked at the disaster and shook his head. He collected the reins of Comet and the painted horses and led them to a large hitching post. The princesses' grand entrance was ruined, and no one paid them any more attention.

Then a tall queen noticed a horse and rider approaching the dance. "Who is that?" she asked loudly.

The crowd went silent again. All eyes turned to see a simple brown horse carrying a lone girl to Sweet Hall. The horse was large and calm. He wasn't wearing a bridle, but he took slow, smooth steps and he was under the complete control of his rider. He carried her with a proud arched neck.

The girl sat very still on his back. She had a sad face, but she didn't seem sad. Her head was held high, and her dress billowed around her. She looked like an angel sitting on a silver cloud.

Caden smiled. "It's Cianna."

"Cianna!" The name rippled through the crowd.

"The blind pet washer?" one royal asked another.

"No, surely this girl is a princess," said a wealthy visitor from Trabor, noticing Cianna's regal posture, beautiful clothing, and well-trained horse.

While the crowd buzzed about the mysterious guest, the Spring Festival artists abandoned their sketches of the princesses and set their easels with fresh paper. They sketched furiously, capturing the perfection of Cianna and Gildon.

Polly scratched her legs and arms, more uncomfortable than ever in her wet, itchy dress. Meanwhile, the crowd parted for Cianna.

Caden pushed through them to help her off Gildon. "I see he found you," Caden said.

"I knew it was you who sent him!" Cianna was relieved to hear a friendly voice. She could tell that everyone was staring at her again.

Caden patted Gildon. He had trained the horse himself, and he was proud.

Princess Polly was confused. She dragged herself over to Cianna. "What are you doing here?"

"I'm here for the dance."

Polly shook her head. The last person she expected to see tonight was Cianna. "I'm sorry, but Mirabel isn't sick anymore. She took her spot back. I was going to tell you, but you ran away."

Cianna held up her two tickets. "I'm not here to dance with you, Polly."

"Oh," Polly said, still confused and upset by her fall.

Cianna had an idea. "Will you go to the dance with me, Caden?"

He looked down at his fancy white carriage suit. He was certainly dressed for it. "Yes, I would like that." He turned to Adeline and Jamie. "May I have your permission to attend the dance with Cianna?"

Adeline and Jamie exchanged a smile. "Of course! You two have fun," said Adeline.

"Excuse us," Cianna said to Polly.

Cianna took Caden's arm, ready to walk away. Just then, Polly's rainbow wriggled violently in her dress.

"What's happening?" Polly cried, looking down.

The rainbow was struggling hard against the white fabric. Polly clutched at her skirt, and she noticed it was torn. The rainbow found the rip in her dress at the same time; it pushed itself out of the fabric and into the air.

The crowd of people jumped back as the rainbow slid out of the dress. It whipped around like a scared snake, and a few royals screamed. The rainbow streamed upward but shrank back at the darkness of the night. Night is a scary time for rainbows; it would have to wait until morning to return to the sky.

Desperate, the rainbow curled through the legs of the terrified crowd. A woman tried to touch it and the rainbow lashed at her. Princess Anna and other guests bolted for the safety of Sweet Hall.

Lexi hid behind a bush, and her mood fabric changed from yellow to blazing red. "Stop it!" she shouted at her gown.

The rainbow zeroed in on Cianna's cloud dress. Cianna could not see what was happening, but she could tell by the screams and the sounds of people running that something was wrong. The rainbow darted toward her. Cianna heard renewed gasps and squeals and the people standing near her skittered away.

Cianna's cloud dress swelled as the rainbow neared, and she smelled rain. She touched her dress—it was damp. The rainbow circled Cianna, nosing the cloud fabric like a cautious animal.

"Don't move," Caden said under his breath.

The frightened rainbow zipped away from Cianna, and then it bunched itself up like a spring, turned, and shot into Cianna's dress. It circled like a dog chasing its tail until finally, it settled calmly into the cloud.

Cianna stood in the center of everyone with her dress radiating color all around her. Her face was awash in bright pastels, her silver highlights blazed, and her green eyes sparkled. She lit up the front lawn like a lamp. No one had ever seen a more beautiful gown. The glow of a content rainbow could not compare to the pale color of a trapped rainbow. A cheer rose up among the royals, and they clapped and hooted. Cianna—still stunned and unsure of what had just happened—did not know what to do. The sketch artists went mad with their pencils.

"Just curtsy," said Caden, amused.

And so she did. She bowed deeply and the crowd burst into a fresh round of applause.

Polly sucked in her breath. She was soaking wet, her hair was flat, and now her rainbow was gone. Blue dye had stained her dress, and she was just a ragged girl wearing itchy sackcloth. No one even noticed her, which was kind of a good thing at this point.

Polly glared at Cianna and Gildon. *She's got my ugliest dress, my plainest horse, and my cheapest jewels*, Polly thought. *Why is she getting all the attention?* She huffed and ran inside to the bathroom. As she ran, one of her glass slippers shattered, cutting her foot. "Ughhhh!" Polly cried.

"My lady, you have stolen the show," whispered Caden in Cianna's ear.

She blushed, and he took her arm. The crowd noticed the proud boy at Cianna's side. He looked regal in his carriage suit. The handsome couple held hands, with Gildon standing obediently behind them. After so many of Cianna's baths, he was the shiniest horse at the dance. No amount of glitter could compare to the brilliant sheen of his healthy coat.

"Why, I never," exclaimed an old queen in delight. "A stable boy and a pet washer—just look at them!"

And everyone did. The younger princes and princesses bowed while Katie untied her harp and played joyful music.

Cianna did not know how wonderful she looked; she was just happy to be at the dance. A stable boy from another castle led Gildon away for his dinner and massage. Cianna and Caden entered the Spring Dance together. Adeline, Jamie, and the crowd followed them into the hall.

Thirteen

~The Spring Dance~

ONCE INSIDE, Cianna was not disappointed. Everything was just as she'd always dreamed it would be. She smelled savory meats, earthy vegetables, exotic seasonings, and luscious fruits. The food scents weaved together a fabric of warmth and goodness.

The royals walked here and there, the scent of their lovely perfumes wafting behind them. Of course, the pets were all washed and scented as well, but Cianna could smell some doggy bad breath. Whoever had washed the pets had not brushed their teeth. *Mr. Talley really needs me*, she thought.

The music sounded better in the big hall than it did from the window in her apartment. It was full and lively. She felt the beat of the drums in her chest, the violins caressed her sensitive ears, and the complex rhythms made her feet tap.

Caden brought her punch and sweets from the buffet tables. Cianna could not believe she was here, and neither could Caden. They didn't know what to do first.

"Will you dance with me?" Caden asked. His confident voice was, for once, uneasy.

"I would like that," Cianna answered, just as nervous.

Caden escorted her onto the floor. He spun her, held her tight, then spun her some more! Caden and Cianna's playfulness was contagious. Soon, Katie joined them. She loved to dance, and she was funny. She entertained them with jokes, and Cianna could not remember the last time she'd laughed so hard.

Meanwhile, there was no sign of Polly, and no one seemed to notice her absence—except, of course, her parents. Jamie and Adeline knew Polly was hiding in the restroom, but they left her alone so she could think.

When Cianna realized Polly wasn't enjoying the dance, she went to look for her. Caden had told her about the firecracker, Tiara throwing Polly into the fountain, and about the rainbow escaping from Polly's dress and finding refuge in Cianna's.

She found Polly sitting alone on the bathroom floor. She sat down next to her and waited for Polly to speak.

"You must hate me," Polly moaned.

"I don't hate you."

"I know we hurt you, Cianna." Polly's voice was grim. "You can be happy now because my night is ruined."

"That doesn't make me happy!"

Polly hugged herself. "I had the best dress, the best horse, the best pet, and the best friends. How did everything go wrong?"

Cianna thought about what she said. "Did you have the best things, Polly?"

"Of course I did," she answered. "I'm not blind." Polly slapped her hand over her mouth. "Oops, sorry."

Cianna laughed. "Well, I can't see, Polly, but I don't agree with you."

"What do you mean?"

"I don't agree that you had the best things," Cianna explained. "Your dress is rough and scratchy. It might look good, but it feels like a potato sack. Your horse doesn't behave, and someday she's going to hurt you. Leroy is sweet, that's true, but he's not a good pet. A dog is supposed to be your best friend, but Leroy only cares about sleeping, and he avoids you."

Cianna reached for Polly's hand. "And your friends, Polly," Cianna shook her head, "well most of them are great, but where are they now?"

Polly looked around. She was alone in the bathroom. Only Cianna had come to check on her.

"Did you know Anna got me suspended from my job?" Cianna asked.

"No!" Polly gasped. "I thought you took a vacation."

Cianna explained what Princess Anna had done to her. Polly was shocked. "I didn't tell her to do that," she said, "and I didn't notice those things about my dress and stuff until everything went wrong."

"There's a lot you don't notice, Polly, maybe it's time you opened your eyes." Cianna let go of her hand and left the restroom.

She returned to Caden and Katie. Caden fetched cake and punch for each of them. Afterward, they danced some more to the lively music.

Polly finally came out of the bathroom. Her dress had dried, and she threw her glass slippers away since one was broken. She rested against a wall and watched the princes and princesses dance. She saw Caden, Cianna, and Katie laughing. Everyone was having fun. Cianna's dress lit up the room. The rainbow was happy in the cloud. Polly knew it would return to the sky in the morning, but for now it stayed with Cianna.

Polly scratched her legs and waist. There was really nothing softer or more comfortable than a cloud dress. She touched her side which was sore from falling off Tiara. Gildon had looked so strong and handsome when he walked up the hill, and he was calm, unlike her mare.

She watched the pets in the room. They kept their eyes on their owners begging for treats and snuggling with them. Trixi stood on her hind legs and danced with Mirabel. Peaches performed a handstand on Anna's shoulder, delighting the crowd, and Lexi shared a whole cherry pie with her bear, Lucy.

Polly spotted Leroy resting on a velvet sofa. She whistled to him. His eyes snapped to hers and then he jumped down and trotted out of the room. Cianna was right, he avoided her.

Polly turned her thoughts to Prince Jayson. He was showing off his medal to all the pretty girls. Nearby, Caden waited on Cianna like a gentleman, and Polly's friends dotted the dancing hall laughing and gossiping. It was like they had all forgotten about her—even little Katie.

Polly couldn't believe how much fun Cianna was having with her old dress, her brown horse, her polite stable boy, and her plain friend. *I have been blind*, she thought. *Not anymore!*

Polly hunted down the princesses. They shrank from her, thinking she was angry. "This isn't about me," Polly said. She *was* angry, but not at them. For the first time in her life, Polly was angry at herself. "We need to talk about Cianna." The girls huddled together while Polly explained her mistakes. "And you"—Polly pointed at Anna—"have a lot to explain to Mr. Talley!"

Anna felt terrible about what she'd done to Cianna and Mr. Talley. She'd only been trying to help, even though Polly hadn't asked her to. She crossed the hall to find the store owner, and they had a long chat.

The princesses settled on a plan, and Polly headed for the stage. When the music ended, Polly took her place in front of the audience. "Ladies and gentlemen," she announced, "my friends will now perform our dance, *The Seven Sisters!*"

Everyone cheered.

One dancer did not take her place—Polly. She cleared her throat, and the crowd quieted to hear her speak again. "I would like to ask a very special girl to take my place tonight. She worked hard to learn *The Seven Sisters*, and she is our friend. Her name is Cianna."

Everyone looked around for Cianna, who was standing by the cookies. "Me?" she asked.

"Yes, you!" Caden chuckled. "Do you want to dance?"

Cianna paused. *Polly is just a young girl, she didn't mean to hurt me.* "Yes, I do want to dance." Caden led her to the stage.

Polly helped her up. "Thank you, Cianna," she whispered, "for everything."

"But I'm not in my costume," Cianna pointed out.

"It's okay," Polly said. "We're together, and that's more important."

Lexi took Cianna's hand. "I'm sorry I was mean," she said. "I thought Polly … that she, well—" Lexi stumbled over the truth. "I thought she liked you better than me. I'm her best friend."

Cianna sensed true regret in Lexi's voice. "It's forgotten," she said.

Lexi squeezed her hand. "Let's knock'em dead!"

Katie strummed her harp and the girls danced *The Seven Sisters.* No one missed a step. Polly sniffled. Her best friends were all together, and the crowd loved the performance. When it was over, the guests threw flowers at the girls. Cianna smelled rose petals.

Polly walked on stage to bow with her dancers. She closed her eyes. "It smells like love," she said.

Cianna giggled. "You learn fast, Polly."

The girls left the stage, and people stood in line to tell them how well they had danced. The last person in line was Mr. Talley.

"Hello, Mr. Talley!" Cianna missed her boss.

"I had a talk with Princess Anna," he said. "She told me what really happened to Peaches."

"She did?"

"Yes, and I'm sorry Cianna. I should have stood up for you. I was wrong."

"It's okay, Mr. Talley, I know you didn't want to suspend me. Peaches lost all his hair; you didn't have a choice!"

"You're wrong, Cianna," Mr. Talley said. "I had a choice. I didn't know what happened to that rat, but I was sure it wasn't your fault." He shook his head. "I was more worried about my best customer than my best employee. Can you forgive me, Cianna?"

She smiled, relieved that the mystery of the hairless rat had been fully resolved. "I forgive you, Mr. Talley."

"And you can have your job back whenever you're ready," he offered, "with a raise of course."

They shook hands. "Thank you!" Cianna said.

Cianna heard Polly and Lexi apologize to Katie for all the times they had left her out. "You are a true friend, Katie," Polly said. "Will you come over and have tea with us next week?"

"I would love to!" Katie answered.

Now the evening is perfect, thought Cianna. She would be sad in the morning when it was all over.

Cianna, Caden, Polly, Katie, Adeline, Jamie, and the princesses danced together for the rest of the night. Prince Jayson didn't mind Polly's horrible dress—he asked her to dance six times! Polly ended up having a wonderful evening.

When it was over, Caden drove them back to the castle in the carriage. Polly and Cianna fell asleep on top of each other like exhausted puppies.

"They could almost be sisters," said Adeline. She and Jamie held hands all the way home.

Fourteen

~Summer~

CIANNA SPENT the next few days with Polly's family. She was in no hurry to return to her lonely apartment. She rode Gildon, attended tea parties, and played games with Polly. King Jamie took the girls fishing, and Adeline took them swimming in the pond. Polly decided to let Caden train Tiara. He rode her every day and already, the mare was behaving better.

The family decided to stay in Windym for another month before leaving for Amerok. They wanted to spend more time with Cianna.

One afternoon Jamie called the family into the grand living room. When they were all seated, he handed Cianna a gift. "This is for you."

Cianna opened the box, and inside was a book. "Um, thanks," she said. Didn't they remember she couldn't read?

Jamie chuckled. "Open the book, Cianna, and you'll understand."

Cianna opened the book. She touched the pages and felt hundreds of tiny bumps under her fingertips. They made elaborate patterns, similar to the ones she scratched on her glass bottles! Cianna's heart raced. "What is this?"

King Jamie explained, "Adeline told me how you mark your bottles with symbols so that you know what's in them. I wondered if this would work for reading words. I hired a team of inventors to develop a reading code. The best bookmakers in the world are from our kingdom in Amerok. They are now making books for blind people."

Cianna was speechless.

Jamie grinned. "I'm bringing a teacher here on my ship. She will show you how to read the symbols. This particular book is about a young girl who can speak to animals. Polly chose it for you. It's one of her favorites."

"Thank you!" Cianna cried. She jumped up and gave King Jamie a huge hug.

"We have something else for you," Adeline said.

This sounded serious. "Okay …" Cianna clutched her new book to her chest.

"We want you to live here, Cianna," the queen said. "We want this castle to be your home."

"Yes," agreed Jamie. "And we'll save a room for you in Amerok too. You can visit whenever you want."

"We'll be like sisters!" Polly gushed.

Cianna wondered if she'd heard right. "You want me to live here, like forever?"

"Forever," said Adeline, "or for as long as you want. You may come and go as you please. Just think about it."

"Take your time," said Jamie.

Cianna didn't need to think about it. "I want to!" she said. Cianna had her own tiny apartment, but it was much nicer to live with other people.

They each jumped out of their chairs and grabbed one another. "You're going to love it here!" Polly cried.

"I already do." Cianna's grin lit up her sad face and melted the queen.

"Let's celebrate!" declared Adeline. "I'll make ice-cream sundaes."

"Great," said Polly. "Let's tell Caden, Cianna."

The two girls held hands and ran to the stable. Leroy followed them. Cianna had changed Leroy's diet, and now he had more energy. Polly stopped dressing him in clothing and started playing fetch and tug-of-war with him instead. Now he followed the princess everywhere she went.

Cianna and Polly told Caden the good news. He grabbed the girls and spun them around.

The three of them laughed until they fell down. As Cianna lay on the stable floor, she smelled the horses, the pigs, and the roses outside. She couldn't believe it. She had a home and a family who loved her.

The kennel dogs heard them having fun and whined. Polly sat up as though struck by lightning. "They need families too!" she cried.

"Who are you talking about, Polly?" asked Cianna.

"My dogs!" Polly howled. "They're lonely in that kennel, that's why they whine. I don't play with them."

"At least they have everything else they need," Cianna said, trying to soothe her friend.

"No," Polly disagreed. "They don't have families."

"Polly is right. Dogs need families too," Caden said.

"What am I going to do?" Polly moaned. "They can't all live in the castle. It would be great if they each had their own child to play with and their own home to live in."

Polly remembered the Country Day School. She'd seen so many kids there, nice kids. Dogs were expensive in Windym because they had to be shipped in from other kingdoms. Raising puppies on the island was not allowed because of its small size. It could too quickly become overrun by dogs. Polly thought of the little toothless first-grade girl. She would probably love to have her own dog. "I know what to do!"

Two weeks later, the King and Queen of Amerok threw a huge party. The children and families from the Country Day School and all of the princes and princesses who were still on the island were invited to attend. At the party, Jamie and Adeline crowned Cianna as an honorary Princess of Amerok. It was more fun than the Spring Dance! Katie played the harp. Mia, Mr. Talley, and Jolee were there, and Adeline baked a three-tier cake with a candy crown on top.

Each child from Country Day School was escorted to Polly's kennel, where they chose their very own dog. Cianna had bathed the dogs with rose shampoo and brushed all their teeth. Polly handed each child the dog of his or her choice. Cianna gave the new owners pretty baskets filled with dog shampoo, doggie toothpaste, minty bones, a large bag of dog food, and a coupon for a free beauty treatment at the Royal Pet Palace and Day Spa— compliments of Mr. Talley!

Polly gave the last dog away to the little first-grade girl. Her name was Bella, and she chose a tiny black puppy. She named him Hopper, and he wriggled in her arms trying to lick her face. Bella thanked Polly and hugged the princess as tight as she could.

Polly burst into tears. "This is so fun, why am I crying?" she asked.

Cianna and Caden laughed at her. When they were finished handing out the dogs, Polly and Cianna returned to the party.

Cianna was munching crackers by the lawn when a hush fell over the crowd. Once again, she felt everyone staring at her. *What now?* Then she heard hoofbeats.

Caden led a horse to Cianna and stopped in front of her. She reached out and felt an arched neck with a satin ribbon tied around it. "He's gift-wrapped," Caden explained.

Cianna's heart sank. "Why?" *Was Polly giving away her horses too, would they give away Gildon!*

King Jamie strode across the patio and stood next to Cianna. "Because he's yours now," Jamie said.

Cianna gasped. "You can't give me a horse!" They had done too much for her already!

"He's always been your horse, Cianna. I'm just making it official."

The horse licked her fingers. *It was Gildon!* Cianna wrapped her arms around him; his hide was warm in the afternoon sun. It truly was the best day of her life.

"Look in the sky!" someone shouted.

Cianna heard a blasting noise. "It's a cloud harvest!" Polly said. At least thirty hot air balloons were drifting across the blue horizon.

"What's that?" asked Cianna.

"They're catching clouds in silver nets to make more cloud dresses," Polly squealed. "You started the trend when you made the cover of *Princess Style* magazine, Cianna."

"It's true," said Mrs. Dunkins with a smile. She was one of the only dressmakers in the seven kingdoms experienced at sewing clouds, and now she was buried in orders for cloud dresses. She would make a tidy profit this year.

"You're kidding!" said Cianna. "I'm a fashion icon?" The thought sent her into a fit of giggles. She laughed until her stomach hurt. Soon everyone joined her even though they didn't know what was so funny.

The following week her new family left for Amerok. Cianna and Caden saw them off at the pier. Polly, Cianna, and Adeline sobbed as they said goodbye. Jamie promised to send a ship in the fall to bring Cianna to Amerok for a visit.

At the dock, Polly and her family boarded the giant ship bound for their homeland. Their trunks were already loaded. Tiara was going with them, and she was in a stall in the cargo area. Leroy walked beside Polly, proud and loyal, like a dog should be.

"I'll miss you, Leroy," Cianna said, patting him.

Polly and Cianna gripped each other in a fierce hug, both with lumps in their throats.

"You're not allowed in my room while I'm gone," Polly joked.

"You're not allowed to collect any more animals," Cianna shot back.

"Take good care of her," Polly ordered Caden.

"Yes, Your Highness."

Cianna and Caden stood on the dock waving until Caden told her the ship was out of sight. The lump in Cianna's throat would not go away. Caden sensed her sorrow. "I'll race you to the Snow Globe," he said.

This made Cianna laugh. "You're on!" They jumped on their horses and galloped all the way to the ice-cream shop. Cianna felt much better after two scoops of chocolate ice cream with extra marshmallows and a cherry on top!

~ ~ ~ ~ ~

Over the long summer Cianna made scented pet shampoos as gifts for her new family and princess friends. She shipped the gifts to each of the seven kingdoms. Word of Cianna's healing soaps spread fast. Soon she was drowning in requests for her products. King Jamie wrote Cianna a letter and encouraged her to start her own business.

She cleaned out her old apartment and turned it into a laboratory. There, Cianna perfected her line of animal soaps, shampoos, toothpastes, medicines, and treats. Her products were so popular that the shopkeepers could not keep them on the shelves. After training a new pet washer for Mr. Talley, Cianna became a full-time business owner.

Jamie and Adeline had chosen a bedroom for Cianna in the castle before they left. They put in soft, thick carpet and painted the walls. Since Cianna didn't care what color it was, she let Polly choose. The princess selected emerald green for the walls and sky blue for the ceiling.

Mia visited the castle every Sunday for dinner. Cianna rode Gildon into town five days a week to work at her lab. On the weekends she and Caden rode their horses through the forests and meadows of Windym just for fun. The teacher came from Amerok, and she taught Cianna how to read in the afternoons. Cianna was content.

In some ways her life hadn't changed at all—she still worked hard, she still was blind, and she still missed her father. But in other ways she would never be the same. Cianna had gained a new family, made new friends, learned to read, become an honorary princess (not to mention a fashion icon), and learned how to ride a horse!

Cianna also learned that people's ability to see their choices didn't correspond with their ability to make good choices. She made good choices, and that made her far less blind than most of her friends.

Cianna was now famous in Windym and the seven kingdoms. Everyone liked to tell the tale of the pet washer who had become a princess. Someday, Cianna decided, she would write down her story herself.

~The End~

About the Author

Jennifer Lynn Alvarez graduated from U.C. Berkeley with a Bachelor of Arts degree in English Literature. She is a full-time author, blogger, speaker, wife, and mother of three.

The Pet Washer is the first in a three-book series chronicling the friendships and adventures of young Cianna.

Please visit www.thepetwasher.com to email Jennifer, take quizzes on the book, post fan fiction, view photos of her pets, and feed her crazy fish!

Jennifer lives in Northern California with her family and their menagerie of animal friends.

Book Two

The Wishing Star

Join Cianna and Caden on a journey across the Azules Ocean! In an attempt to win a wish on the Wishing Star, Caden and his colt, Dash, risk life and limb in a brutal horse race.

Cianna supports them every step of the way with special grain for Dash and encouragement for Caden.

But can a stable boy win a race against men? Can an untried colt win a race against stallions? And if they succeed, what in the world will Caden wish for?

JENNIFER LYNN ALVAREZ
www.thepetwasher.com

CPSIA information can be obtained at www.ICGtesting.com
Printed in the USA
LVOW08s2048060315

429542LV00001B/73/P